MEANT-TO-BE
MOTHER

MEANT-TO-BE MOTHER

BY

ALLY BLAKE

MILLS & BOON®

First published in Great Britain 2006
Large Print edition 2007
Harlequin Mills & Boon Limited,
Eton House, 18-24 Paradise Road,
Richmond, Surrey TW9 1SR

© Ally Blake 2006   GW 28396510

ISBN-13: 978 0 263 19454 8
ISBN-10:   0 263 19454 X

Set in Times Roman 17¼ on 19¾ pt.
16-0507-50538

Printed and bound in Great Britain
by Antony Rowe Ltd, Chippenham, Wiltshire

To my gorgeous genius of a godson, Lachlan.
Hugs and kisses from your Auntie Ally.

CHAPTER ONE

S<small>IENA</small> C<small>APULETTI</small> was going home.

And where for most people that would bring about happy thoughts of familiar faces, their own bed and their favourite pillow, the concept had poor Siena in a cold sweat.

Well, okay, so the wet clammy feeling could also have come from the fact that she had just been on the receiving end of a well-flung can of cola courtesy of a pouting kid in the aeroplane seat next to her.

But still…clammy was clammy. Uncomfortable. Hot and cold all at once. Nope. It was definitely thoughts of *home* making her feel that way. Home just didn't bring about warm and fuzzy feelings in Siena.

The splotch of insidious brown beverage inching its way across her Dolce and Gabbana skirt and matching jacket—the only 'interview outfit' she had packed for her short trip to her provincial home town—grew larger and overtook the proportion of clean cream tweed.

'Excellent,' she said under her breath.

Siena craned her head past the rows of seats as she flapped her sticky outfit away from her damp body. Where was a flight attendant when she needed one? Nowhere. That's where.

It was a sign. She wasn't meant to be heading to Cairns on that day *seated* on a plane; she ought to have been suited up in her usual baby-blue skirt suit, matching pillbox hat and beige high heels, working the aisle as a Cabin Director for MaxAir rather than finding herself at the mercy of one.

But when Maximillian Sned, the eccentric septuagenarian owner of MaxAir—the funky, cosmopolitan, fun-and-games airline for which she worked—had summoned her to meet him to discuss a 'fabulous career move'—his words—at his palatial home north of Cairns, what choice had she had? Even though, if the rumour mill was correct, and let's face it, it usually was, his offer was going to entail a *fabulous move* to Cairns to stay.

Double excellent.

A hard kick to the shins brought Siena back to the less than pleasant present.

Blithely ignoring the pint-sized, cola-flinging, kick-boxing champ to her left, Siena tried to remember the meditation class she had once taken—close your eyes, take deep calming breaths and think of a happy place. A beach hut in Hawaii? A Swiss ski resort? That shoe shop on Madison Avenue she couldn't walk into without spending a week's pay?

But Siena was surprised to find she could barely recollect the shapes and colours and sensation of being anywhere but the inside of a plane—

'I am soooooo sorry it took me so long! We have a guy in the back row who can juggle soft drink cans. Seriously, soft drink cans! He was teaching me and I *almost* had it down.'

Siena opened one eye to find a perky, blonde, perfectly groomed flight attendant with 'Jessica' scrawled on to her name badge. She smiled prettily as she handed over a baby-blue box of MaxAir brand moist towels to Siena and another drink to the pouting kick-boxer at Siena's side.

Her vague happy place feelings slipped away to naught as Siena realised her day was not about to get any better.

Seven years as a sky girl and Siena could read people at first glance. She knew which passenger would try to sneak an illegal cigarette puff in the bathroom, which one would be a white knuckle flyer who would need a Bloody Mary as soon as they took off, and which one would try to pinch every female bottom and thus would be fast shifted to a window seat.

Jessica had just given the kid beside her a *new* can of cola. Crayons and warm milk would have been the better option. Siena could read that Jessica was sweet but entirely hopeless.

She wondered briefly if she ought to let Maximillian know when she met him. But no. Siena didn't do meddling. Growing up with a brother twelve years her senior shoving unwanted advice down her neck her whole life had cured her of that.

'Now, Freddy,' Jessica cooed, 'this time we have a cool bendy straw in the can so you can suck it up without spilling a drop.'

Spilling? That whole move earlier had nothing do with spilling!

Once Freddy was sucking away, Jessica smiled at Siena in apology. 'You look awfully familiar,' she said. 'Do we know each other?'

Here we go again… Siena was used to being recognised. For the past year her symmetrical, clear-skinned face had been smiling from bill-boards above motorways all over the country advertising the supreme, sassy, fun-in-the-air customer service one could expect from a MaxAir flight. For a small gig that had taken an hour in a photographic studio near her apartment in Melbourne, she suddenly feared it might well change the course of her life.

Would Max really offer the promotional gig on a full-time basis, thus meaning a permanent move to Cairns as everyone expected? If he insisted, would she really have to turn her back on the company that had completely moulded her since she left school?

Her identity, her friendships and her entire life were so intertwined with her job she so hoped it wouldn't come to that, but then a move back to Cairns was utterly, sincerely, outright not an option…

'Maybe from a work Christmas party,' Siena said, telling the truth but skirting the issue all the same. 'I'm a sky girl for Max too. On the international runs.'

'Oh, okay!' Jessica bubbled. 'That must be it. Are you on annual leave or is it just a week-ender to the beach?'

If she mentioned her job interview word would be all over the Far North Queensland operation before they hit the tarmac. 'My brother and his family live in Cairns,' Siena said. 'They just had a new baby.' She kept back the fact that she hadn't ever met Rick's four-year-old twins either.

'Gee,' Jessica said, and, 'wow!'

But Siena could tell the girl wasn't *really* listening. Siena only hoped for the airline's sake that she was still new.

'Okay then, well, happy trails,' Jessica said, her eyes searching out the juggler in the back row again already.

'Happy trails,' Siena parroted back the MaxAir motto.

She watched Jessica bounce her way back down the skinny domestic aisle, her French tipped fingernails clawing on to the backs of passengers' seats for balance and her blonde ponytail bouncing.

Siena blinked. It had been a long while since she had mastered the ability to walk an aisle in two-inch heels without needing a thing to help her balance.

She was a pro. A lifer. Born to fly. Far far away…

If only Max saw that she could be more to the company than a smiling face on a bill-board. If only the rumour mill had Max offering her Rome.

Siena sighed and slid further down in her seat. She took a deep breath and closed her eyes. Cool, cosmopolitan Rome was at the heart of the MaxAir international routes. The top of the heap. The pièce de résistance. Now *that* would be a *fabulous career move*.

The hum of the engine altered and Siena knew the plane was descending. She looked out the small window to see hilly green land undulating down to twisting white sands and deep blue water peeking back at her from between patchy white cloud cover. Tropical Cairns. Paradise. *Home…*

Siena peeled her clamped fingers from the armrests and shook life back into them.

Okay, you have a few minutes, now deep breathe and focus on happy thoughts.

As the overhead lights called for everyone to do up their seat belts, Siena toed her fake red Kelly handbag further under her seat. Shopping in Hong Kong was a happy place. Why hadn't she conjured that thought? Next time. And she had a feeling she would be needing many of those *next times* over the coming weekend.

Out of the corner of her eye, Siena noticed

that young Freddy was sitting staring at his open seat belt with one half in each of his hands as his cola balanced precariously between his knobbly knees. He had a cola moustache on his upper lip and beads of sweat stood out on his forehead. But her friendly neighbourhood flight attendant was nowhere to be seen.

What sort of parents deemed him independent enough to look out for himself at the age of five? She'd seen it time and again in her job and had never been able to understand such thought processes. *She* of all people knew just how such an assumption of early independence could turn the poor kid—hostile, erratic, doing anything and everything to get attention. To get discipline. To get a parent to tell him no.

She found herself experiencing an unexpected moment of empathy. Well, the kid hadn't spilt anything on her in the last five minutes and she had to give him kudos for that.

'Would you like me to help you with that?' she found herself asking.

'Yes, please,' the boy said with a cherubic lisp.

Siena shuffled in her seat and took a hold of the two halves of the seat belt. The young boy lifted his thin arms and Siena had a whiff of something sweet like a mix of cola and biscuits.

When the belt clicked into place he gave a little sniff and Siena realised that two tracks of shiny tears were sliding down his cheeks. Oh, heck. A sniffly kid, and now tears? Was she being punished for something?

In the end empathy won out again. For the next fifteen minutes she talked the kid down from his cola high, and up from his lonely low, so that when the plane landed, and Jessica and her bouncing ponytail took him away, she was sure that he had been replaced by a completely different kid.

Siena waited until the plane was all but empty to grab her carry-on and suit bag containing her uniform for the working flight back to Melbourne on Saturday evening. She wasn't in any hurry.

When she disembarked on to the tarmac the Far North Queensland heat hit her like a slap in the face. The air was thick, hot and wet. She could taste her own sweat on her lips. The tangy scent of the nearby sea hung heavy in the air. She could feel her dark curls frizzing by the second, her feet sweating in her designer shoes and the cola in her dress weighing her down as all evaporation ceased in the humid air.

Inside the thankfully air-conditioned terminal, a wiry silver-moustachioed man in a three-piece suit and hat in MaxAir's incongruous powder-blue, completely unsuitable in the temperate climate, stood waiting with a sign reading 'CAPULETTI'.

A driver? Max was pulling out the big guns. But, though it was a nice gesture, it only made Siena's heart sink all the further.

'I'm Siena Capuletti,' she said, approaching slowly.

The man nodded. 'Rufus,' he said in a deep baritone. 'Maximillian has asked that I be at your disposal for the weekend, Ms Capuletti.'

'Right. Well. Excellent.' Siena moved into the flow of the crowd, making her way through the backwater 'international' terminal, along tracts of unfashionable carpet long since in need of updating. She kept Rufus, who'd insisted on taking her baggage, in the corner of her vision. He had a look about him that made Siena think that if she pointed at another passenger and said, 'Kill,' he wouldn't have any trouble obeying.

'I have to make a quick call,' she told him just before they left the air-conditioning. Rufus stopped where he stood like a dog who had been told to *stay*, though he had all the warmth of a German Shepherd police dog.

Siena found a quiet corner and made the call she had been dreading for days.

'Hello,' her brother Rick's deep voice rumbled.

For a moment she thought about hanging up. Why did she have to tell him she was back? It was a flying visit anyway. He didn't even have her mobile number, so he wouldn't even know it was her—

'Anyone there?' he asked, and Siena gave in.

'Rick, it's Siena.'

After a long pause he came back to her.

'Well, well, well. *Piccolo*. It's been some long while since I have heard your lovely voice.'

Rick's passive aggressive comment was almost enough to have Siena switching off her phone and turning right around.

'*Una momento*,' Rick said, and she heard a crash of something kitcheny followed by the shouts of two young boys in the background. It gave her a moment to recollect herself.

'Michael! Leo! Stop that,' Rick's voice cried somewhere near the phone. 'Sit at the table and your mama will bring your cereal in a second. Sorry, *Piccolo*, breakfast is like a battle zone around here. So where are you today? Paris? London?'

Here goes… 'I'm at the Cairns Airport.'

She was met with deathly silence. It seemed he was as shocked that she was back after all this time as she was.

'Well, I'll be… Our little bird has returned to the nest. Does this mean I get to see your pretty face for real, not just on those big posters near the airport?'

Siena closed her eyes and leant her forehead

against her fist. 'I'm here until Saturday evening, so, sure. Why not? I have a meeting with Maximillian tomorrow afternoon but, apart from that, this little bird is, well, as free as a bird.'

'Great. Tell me which terminal and I'll pick you up.'

'No, it's okay. I have a driver.' She felt a mix of pride and stupidity in admitting as much and she cringed as she awaited Rick's usual unimpressed laughter. But it never came.

'But you *are* staying here,' he said, not even a hint of a question in his commanding tone. 'Tina can make up the spare room.'

She thought of the big king-sized bed and Egyptian cotton sheets that would be awaiting her at the suite Max had organised for her at the Novotel Resort in the beachside haven of Palm Cove, and imagined the chintz comforter, sagging single bed and recriminations no doubt awaiting her at the Capuletti home. Hmm, tough decision.

'Come,' he said, hearing her pause. 'Stay with us. Please. I'm not asking the world of you, Siena, but it is more than time you met your nephews and niece.'

Siena used her spare hand to rub away her frown. It was the *please* that got her. She couldn't remember a time when she had ever heard that word come from Rick. *Ever.* She was more used to: *Do this. Be that. If you don't, one of these days you'll give poor Papa a heart attack...*

'Sure,' she said, her throat tight with emotion. 'But only for a couple of days. I'm in town on a purpose and this meeting tomorrow is really important—'

'A couple of days would be wonderful, *Piccolo.*'

Siena nodded even though he couldn't see her.

'Do you have our new address?' he asked.

Siena was embarrassed to realise she had no idea. She knew they had sold the family home a few years before. Her half of the money from its sale was still sitting untouched, unwelcome, gathering interest and dust, in a bank account. But she hadn't a clue where they were living now.

'You may as well give it to me again,' she said, reaching into her handbag for her PDA.

Rick reeled off his suburban address in a new estate Siena hadn't even heard of and she typed it in under his name. Well, it had been seven years since she'd lived there…

'We're heading off soon to take the kids to Tina's mother's for the day, then we both have to work, but we'll leave you a key under the mat. Make yourself at home.'

Home. Again that small word clenched at deep dark places inside Siena's chest as suppressed visions of the old family house took root in the corner of her mind.

'I'll see you later tonight?' Rick asked.

'See you then.' She hung up and turned to find Rufus watching her quietly. He approached, making a dead-straight beeline through the departing crowd.

'Straight to Palm Cove, then, Ms Capuletti?'

'Change of plan, Rufus. Unfortunately Palm Cove is going to be a no go.'

'But Maximillian—'

'I can always catch a cab if it's too much

trouble,' she said, staring him down. Siena could read people in a heartbeat and, though she figured this guy had secrets she didn't even want to know about, she knew that pleasing Max's guests was now priority number one.

He raised one thick silver eyebrow, as though asking if she was going to be this stubborn all weekend. She grinned back at him.

For Siena stubborn was a promise.

An hour later Siena made plans for Rufus to pick her up the next day for her interview, took his business card in case she needed him for anything—car trips, tourist outings, dinner reservations, hits on annoying family members—and let herself into Rick's home.

It was just as she had expected. Within the freshly painted walls of the brand new house lived ancient mismatched furniture from the old family home mixed with assorted Ikea decor. And there was an inherent scent of tomato pasta on the air.

Family pictures littered the top of their old

piano, its keys yellowed by time. Memories crowded in on her as she remembered Rick forcing her to practice at that very piano every single night. While her friends had been at the mall or going to movies, from the day he'd become her legal guardian she had been chained to her weekly routine like a prisoner serving out a sentence for a heinous crime.

Siena lumbered up the stairs, dragging her small case into the obvious spare bedroom where she found a set of keys and a note reading: 'The keys are for the green car. Dinner's at seven.'

After changing into a thankfully cola-free filmy sleeveless black top and skinny dark designer jeans, she searched the Yellow Pages for the name of a dry cleaner. Grabbing her grimy suit and the keys for the green car—not wanting to bother poor Rufus for a quick trip to town, especially since she wasn't entirely sure if she was partial to him or if she was slightly scared of him—she headed out.

The innocuous sounding *green car* turned out to be a great, hulking, Kermit-green, eight-cylinder Ute which looked so neat and sparkly clean it couldn't have been used to haul anything more gritty and cumbersome than plants for Tina's garden.

She started up the monster, took a few moments to familiarise herself with the feel of the pedals as it was the first right-hand-drive car she had driven in months, then backed out of the driveway.

She had to admit it was a beautiful day. Hot and sunny, like every day in Cairns—a huge tourist destination, poised on the edge of the magnificent Great Barrier Reef, one of the seven wonders of the natural world. It really was paradise. For some. For others the hot air felt heavy, smothering, suffocating…

She switched on the air-conditioning, her breathing coming easier when the car smelt less like the past and more like the inside of a plane.

After about five minutes of driving Siena passed an intersection with an antique shop on one corner and an antiquated milk bar on the other and felt a massive wave of *déjà vu*.

Ignoring the map on the display of her PDA, she took a right turn down a familiar-feeling suburban street, shady with gigantic overhanging gum trees. The stillness of the place washed over her as she meandered deeper along the windy road past lovely large two-storey homes with gables and shutters and front porches and grassy front gardens. It was a picture postcard neighbourhood for a young family.

But familiarity soon morphed into prickly realisation.

This was her old street. The home she had lived in for the first eighteen years of her life. The home in which she had grown up as a late child with a bossy older brother and an absentee father…

She rumbled down the street in second gear. Piano music pealed from one house, making her feel giddy. She peered at numbers on letterboxes to draw her focus elsewhere.

And then she found it. Fourteen Apple Tree Drive. Even the street name was picture perfect. But she knew that the lives going on behind such façades weren't anywhere near perfect.

A flash of movement loomed at the corner of her vision and she looked up from the letterbox to see a kid riding his bike out into the street.

Swearing loudly, she slammed on the brakes, the big car tugging and shuddering as she held on for all her might. But her unpractised arms couldn't keep the car straight.

The wheels locked and skidded sideways and, with a crunching jolt, she mounted the kerb. The car slammed to a halt when it came face to face with a hundred-year-old tree in a mass of screeching tyres, grinding metal undercarriage on concrete gutter and the acrid smell of burnt rubber.

Siena's shallow breaths couldn't dull the sound of her thudding heart.

Then she remembered the kid on the bike. She looked through the windscreen.

Nothing.

She looked out the driver's window, then craned her neck to see over her shoulder to the road behind.

Neither child nor bicycle were anywhere to be seen.

CHAPTER TWO

JAMES was sure he heard the screech of car tyres over the sound of his electric sander. He let the sander whirr to a slow stop and whipped his protective goggles to the top of his head.

He stared through the sun-drenched dust floating in the air about him in his backyard workshop, listening.

But there was nothing bar the regular sounds of suburbia—a creaky Hills Hoist clothes-line twirling in the tropical breeze, noisy miner birds fighting over scraps, an amateur pianist a few houses over practising his scales…

He must have imagined it.

His hand moved back to the goggles on his head, ready to get back to work, when he heard a car door slam in his front garden.

He was out of his workshop and sprinting

down the driveway before his work gloves even hit the ground.

The first thing he saw was a green Ute mounted halfway up the kerb, its driver's side door open wide, its front bumper crunched in against his front tree and a soft wisp of smoke spiralling from the bonnet.

The second thing he saw was Kane's bike lying on its side on the street behind the car.

The image ripped through him like someone tearing a photograph in half. If Kane was taken from him too…

Determined to just know, his numb feet took him to the kerb, and once there he saw enough to stop him from thinking such dreadful thoughts.

Kane sat on the road, leaning back against the far side of the car. He was alive. He was animated. And he was talking to a young woman who was crouching down in front of him, running frantic hands over his limbs and head.

A slight young woman with shaggy brown curls finishing just below her ears. A gauzy sort of black top sat high on her back as she crouched, revealing a wide band of olive skin above the waistline of her tight dark jeans.

James stared at the skin, realising in a completely unexpected flash of awareness that it was the first time he had seen that part of a woman's anatomy in an age.

James brought the disturbing thought and his feet to a very definite stop with a crunch of work boot on gravel.

Kane looked over, his pale brown eyes widening as he saw that he and his new friend weren't alone. Instant tears ensued as though the magnitude of what had happened was only realised once James was there to witness it.

'Dad?' Kane said, his high voice cracking.

'I'm here now,' James said as he willed his feet to pick up where they had left off.

One step at a time, he repeated in his head with each footfall.

He had no idea where he had picked up such a mantra—Kane's varied counsellors, late night Internet browsing or even Dr Phil—but it seemed the right mantra for that moment.

He moved towards his son, still not ready to find blood or pain or cracked bones. 'Buddy, are you okay?'

Kane nodded and stood as though he knew James needed to see that he was in one piece. 'I'm fine. I scraped my arm but, as I told Siena, it hardly hurts.'

At the mention of the woman's name, James looked back to find her face drawn with apprehension, her thin eyebrows arched into a frown, her stunning ocean-green eyes wide and blinking and a full lower lip hooked guiltily beneath her two front teeth.

She wiped shaking hands down her tight jeans as she stood, her slim legs wobbling on ridiculously high fire-engine-red pointy heels. Why anyone would drive in such contraptions he had no idea. He fought down a sudden urge to tell her exactly that. To yell, to let loose with every thought that was streaming through his frantic mind, to twist his recent fright back into much more comforting anger.

But every thought that crossed his mind

flitted across her remarkable face and he knew that he didn't have to. He saw mortification. Embarrassment. Something else so quick he missed it, but he caught the tail-end of it through a brief flash of pink across her cheeks.

And then, with an almost imperceptible shake of her head, he recognised the moment she reached the 'get over yourself and go talk to the guy' phase.

'I'm Siena Capuletti,' she said in a lilting voice, holding out a thin hand.

'James Dillon,' he said in return, moving to her to shake.

Her hand was warm. And almost impossibly delicate. This was a hand that had known more manicures than manual labour. For the first time ever he actually felt self-conscious of the work-hardened calluses marring his own large hands.

He let go first but she whipped her hand back with equal speed. As she tucked it into the back pocket of her dark low-rise jeans, James caught a flash of flat tanned stomach.

His insubordinate gaze flickered upward, but

he then had to contend with those eyes. Big, green, framed by the darkest thickest lashes he had ever seen. Suddenly he wasn't quite sure where to look.

'This is my car,' the woman said, pointing at the green Ute when he said nothing. 'Well, it's my brother Rick's. I would never buy a T-shirt in such a colour, much less a sixty thousand dollar car. I was only going slowly, thank goodness, but I didn't see Kane until he was upon me and when I did I braked as hard as my size sevens would allow, and I swerved, and I missed him completely.'

Suddenly she turned at the waist and pinned Kane with a stare. 'You are quite sure I missed you completely?'

Kane nodded earnestly, watching Siena with extreme interest, and James could see that the kid was as captivated as he was himself.

'Oh, thank God,' she continued, crossing herself with a flourish. 'This car is just so bloody big and powerful and…excuse my French. I think I may have hurt your gutter and I have definitely hurt the car and Rick is going to kill me but I will, of course, pay for any damage to your garden, or driveway, or tree or anything.'

It took James a few moments to realise she had come to the end of her speech. He looked back down at Kane, who was now leaning beside the car, sniffling but no longer crying. He was cradling his elbow but, of the two of them, James was pretty certain Siena Capuletti had come out of it the more afflicted of the pair.

James offered the woman a smile by way of acceptance of her apology. Thankful for the reprieve, she smiled back, her eyes glittering like the sun off the coral-laden waters off Green Island.

He stamped out his own smile before his imagination got the better of him. He leant over and picked up the bike and rested it against his thighs, creating a wall between himself and the winsome stranger.

'If Kane says you missed him,' he said, 'then you missed him. He shouldn't have been riding out on to the road as it is.'

She shook her head, her riotous dark curls swishing about her ears. 'I should have been more careful, especially driving down a suburban street.'

She looked up at his house, staring at it for a few moments, her face haunted, overly so he believed, considering how little damage had been done to either person.

She swallowed and then looked back over at him, her big green eyes blinking nineteen to the dozen. He couldn't help himself—he just stared right on back. Was it because she was familiar? Perhaps she lived locally and he had seen her at the supermarket.

No. That wasn't it. He had never seen this woman before. But there was definitely *something* tugging at him. Something potent enough that he found a sudden need to drag his eyes away and down to Kane.

'Now, what have you done to your arm, buddy?'

Kane twisted his arm to show him the nasty scrape. And blood. Seeing blood dribbling down Kane's arm clouded James's mind until he felt as if he was watching the world through a pinhole.

At the behest of each and *every* counsellor who had drifted in and out of Kane's life over the past year—the first recommended by the hospital, yet another organised through Kane's school and even a private one who James thought smelled of his old gym bag but Kane liked him and that was recommendation enough—James had pared his life back to one core mission: devoting himself to Kane. To protect him. To keep him safe. To shield him from *all* further pain. So how the hell had he allowed *this* to happen?

'Maybe we should whip you down to the emergency room to make sure.'

As soon as the words left his mouth James knew it had been exactly the wrong thing to say. Kane's pale eyes grew as big as saucers and his face lost the last vestiges of colour.

Damn it! Over a year of being a single dad and he still managed to find new and interesting ways of screwing it up.

The last time the poor kid had seen his mother

she had been in the care of a pair of smiling ambulance drivers on her way to the hospital for tests. And she had never come home.

James ran a quick hand back and forth over his short hair. This wasn't the time for all that. Late at night, while Kane slept, he could kick himself for any mistakes he'd made before and since to his heart's content, but in daylight hours it was all about keeping Kane on an even keel.

'What was I thinking?' he said, bending down until he was at eye level with his son. He reached out and tucked his hand behind Kane's thin neck. 'A bit of Dettol and a bandage ought to do it. It might sting a bit, but you can take it, can't you, Buddy?'

Kane nodded, the fear in his eyes dampening. ''Course I can.'

'I know first aid,' a modest voice said from behind them. 'Only last week I took my yearly refresher course.'

James turned to find Siena shuffling from one high-heel-shod foot to the other, wringing her slender hands together so hard he could see her knuckles turning white.

'This is entirely my fault,' she said, decreasing the distance between the two of them until she was close enough that he could smell her perfume. Subtle. Expensive. Drinkable. 'Please let me make it up to you.'

Her stormy eyes beseeched him and in that moment he could not remember what she was referring to. A moment was all it was, but that moment was significant. For in that moment he had no memory. No memory of sadness, or loss, or a life put on hold. All he knew in that moment was the exact colour of her eyes.

He wiped the back of his hand across his hot forehead and was not at all surprised to find fresh beads of sweat had gathered there and they had little to do with the Cairns weather. Tropical temperatures he was used to; this unfamiliar woman he was not.

Worried that she was about to fret herself into a dead faint on his front lawn, and knowing she couldn't go anywhere in the Ute as it was, James gave in.

'Come on in out of the heat. I'll call

someone to check out your car. I think we could all do with a cool drink of lemonade.'

James held out an arm and Kane leant against him without argument. He tucked Kane's slight warm body against him and took the wobbly bike up the driveway, not quite sure how it had come to be that he of all people had invited a perfect stranger into his house when even his closest friends had not been inside those walls in months.

Siena ran around to the open driver's side door, quickly shoved her PDA into her handbag and slammed the door shut. She didn't bother locking it; at that point if anyone wanted to try to drive the car away they were welcome to it.

She then found herself following a stranger and his son into Fourteen Apple Tree Drive.

Shock. The only reason she was even contemplating walking into *that* house again had to be shock.

So why wasn't she just waiting by the car while the guy called her a cab and a tow truck so that she and her wobbly legs could be on their way? She had somewhere else to be. She had a Dolce and Gabbana suit fermenting on the back seat of her car, for goodness' sake! She even had Rufus's business card floating about the bottom of her handbag, and she was certain he could be at her side faster than any cab.

But no. For some reason she was following this man into her house...*his* house, for *lemonade*, when she could really do with a strong gin and tonic to calm her seriously taut nerves.

She intently ignored the curved driveway her father had poured the year she'd turned nine and the black shutters on the second floor which she had broken twice when trying to climb out the window after curfew.

Instead she kept her gaze tight on the back of a dusty black T-shirt stretched across a broad back, patches of hair on tanned muscular arms glowing in dappled sunshine, scruffy back pockets of worn old jeans moulded to the lean lines of long legs.

As she neared her father's beloved rose bushes, which she had deflowered completely to load on his breakfast tray one Father's Day, Siena focused as close as someone could on the back of James's neck where short ash-brown hair had been recently shaved into a perfectly straight line revealing a strong tanned neck with a couple of sexy crinkles thrown in for good measure.

Okay, so this was wasn't going to be easy. But did she really need to be focused on sexy neck creases and moulded jeans to get her through? The guy was a *father*, for goodness' sake. No wedding ring—like any self-respecting single woman she had noted that the moment she had seen the guy. But he was definitely the antithesis of what she normally preferred in the male friends she made on her brief stints in different countries around the world.

She liked men in suits. Clean-shaven, single men with time and money and ambition who knew what they wanted and went after it. Men not unlike her.

If her first impression was spot on, and it always was, this guy was a labourer of some sort; the rough pads on the palms of his hands had given that away.

But, remarkably for her, that was as much as she had figured about him. Whether on purpose or through circumstance, this one had a pretty solid wall shielding strangers from seeing too far past that half-smile of his.

Nevertheless she *could* tell that he was covered in what looked like sawdust, he was way too polite for the likes of her and he lived in Cairns. Therefore he was utterly out of bounds.

As they reached the front door, James casually kicked off his work boots to reveal black socks with matching holes in the toes. Kane then held on to the other side of the doorway and mirrored James's actions pre-cisely, pulling off his sneakers by the heel using the toes of his opposite foot.

From nowhere Siena was hit with a wave of vulnerability that was almost stronger than the apprehension repelling her from going inside her childhood home. The charming scene touched her, creating a ball of something entirely new deep in her stomach.

It felt a heck of a lot like longing, but for this focused, no-strings-attached, jet-setting career girl *that* was unlikely.

Maybe it was nausea. She'd been in a car accident after all! Surely such a thing would make anyone a little woozy around the edges and it would explain the wobbly knees, intense interest in the backs of strangers' necks and weird cravings cramping at her innards.

When she stopped in the shade of the portico, the object of her woozy feelings smiled at her—the same odd half-smile he had afforded her earlier. Up close and personal, his smile didn't seem so free and easy—it was cool, aloof, barely reaching his slate-grey eyes. Suddenly she wasn't so sure that she had been sensing the ghosts of her own childhood when driving by this house after all.

'Da-a-ad,' Kane said, tugging on James's arm, and it was enough for his smile to kick up a bare notch, a sliver, a millimetre, but even that tiny alteration turned some sort of switch inside him. And inside her.

With that new low burning light came flecks

of the palest blue into James Dillon's grey eyes, a captivating crease appeared from nowhere in his carved right cheek, and suddenly Siena couldn't remember what she had been worrying about in the first place.

'Come on in. We don't bite,' James said, bathing her in the affectionate smile meant for his son. He then turned and followed his son into the house, leaving the door open for her to follow.

She had to go ahead with this. There was no way she wanted to feel beholden to these guys. Or guilty for almost running the kid down. Especially not guilty. She'd swum through enough of that to know one could never come out clean at the other side.

If she could confiscate cellphones from *Fortune 500* CEOs, tell sheikhs to sit down and shut up and show million-dollar football players how to use their airsickness bags, she could do this.

With a determined flourish she kicked off her red Jimmy Choos, tucked them neatly against the doorway with a quick prayer to the fashion gods that no suburban housewife with a discerning eye for designer footwear might happen by, and with her hot bare feet curling against the cool tiled floor she followed him inside.

Her feet slowed once she realised that, though on the outside she never would have mistaken her old home, on the inside the ground floor was absolutely nothing like it had once been.

Whereas the home she grew up in had been dark and overstuffed with fake Italian statues, old furnishings and too many rugs, James Dillon's home was like the perfect summer day. Buttermilk-yellow walls, soft cream carpet and a collection of the most beautiful highly polished wooden chairs and side tables and cupboards created the illusion of endless space. Walls had been knocked down to create an open flow throughout a house which to her had always felt claustrophobic. She could see all the way through to skylights and bronze hanging pots in the spotless white and wood kitchen and a sunroom had been added to the back of the house, housing a small cane sofa overloaded with scatter cushions.

Finding herself alone, she wandered to a shiny black piano, eerily situated exactly where hers had once been. And, just like hers, it housed a bunch of framed photos scattered across the closed lid.

She laid her red handbag on the piano lid and leant in to get a closer look.

James now wore his brown hair short with a sprinkle of ash throughout, but in the main photo he had longer hair curling about his face, he wore frayed shorts and a T-shirt and had Kane thrown over his shoulder as they ran down a tract of perfect white sand at the beach. She sighed, recognising the landscape as Palm Cove—the peaceful little hamlet where she ought to have been if Rick hadn't guilted her into staying with him in the 'burbs.

Her eyes devoured other photos in which James fished, jumped from planes and taught Kane how to ice-skate. And, in all of the photos, he was smiling. All big white teeth, pink wind-burned cheeks and crinkling blue-grey eyes.

'Well, there you go,' she said aloud, her voice echoing in the lofty space. Whereas polite, quiet James of the half-smiles and worn clothes was a looker, Action James was a true blue—no doubting it—gorgeous son of a gun.

Siena gulped down a strange thickness in her throat. The very fact that she was thinking such thoughts about some guy with a kid should have sent her walking out of the house then and there.

As her hand reached for the handle of her bag and her itchy feet made a move to do just that, Siena suddenly caught sight of a photo of a woman hidden amongst the two dozen of Kane and James. She reached in and took it in her hand.

Sunlight gleamed off thick tousled blonde hair. Rows of neat white teeth beamed from a wide smile. Brown bedroom eyes looked not at the camera but at the person behind the lens.

'Siena?' James said from somewhere out of sight.

'Coming!' she called out, quickly placing the photo back on to the piano lid.

'Through here,' he called back.

She followed the sound of his voice and found Kane sitting on a closed toilet seat while

James was on his haunches searching through a cupboard in an airy bright white downstairs bathroom where her dingy old laundry room had once been.

And, though there was a picture of a beautiful blonde on his piano, and she had almost hit his son with her car, and she had somewhere else to be, and it was none of her business, she couldn't help taking a moment to reconcile James with the guy in the photographs.

Okay, so there was definite gorgeousness still there, only in sepia rather than full Kodak-colour. He looked up to find her staring at him and his grey eyes flickered and narrowed.

Siena blinked several times over, before doggedly turning her attention to the job at hand. Around a dozen different antiseptic creams, lotions and bandages lay on the wide bench top at his side.

'Are you bunking in for a nuclear winter?' she blurted out.

'Somehow I don't think this part of the world is at the top of the nuclear hit list, if it ever comes to that,' he returned, his voice unexpectedly laced with sarcasm. And, since Siena was quite partial to a bit of that herself, she felt her stomach flutters returning.

'Fine. But then what's with the personal pharmacy?' she shot back.

'I'm thorough. Is there something wrong with that?'

'Hey, I'm not complaining. Only a silly woman would put down thoroughness. Just making an observation.'

James's brow furrowed ever so slightly, his mouth hooked up at one corner, and he blinked long and slow. And, just like that, she sensed the game was on.

'And what else have you observed?' he asked, moving to sit back on his haunches, one muscular arm leaning casually along the top of the cupboard door.

She glanced at a much safer Kane, who was watching her with big sad puppy dog eyes, completely trusting. 'Well, I've learned that it's always the big strapping ones who fall apart at the sight of a bit of blood. Now, are you going to sit there with your head in the cupboard all day or will you just move over and let me do it?'

She gave James a little shove on the shoulder and he duly stood and moved to the far side of the room. She then grabbed a bottle of familiar brown liquid, which Rick had preferred when Siena the tomboy had come inside crying after getting in the middle of scrappy fight with local boys.

She felt the temperature in the room change as James moved to sit on the tiled edge of a neat oval spa bath—watching her.

'If I drop a dollop on this perfect white floor,' she said, not looking his way, 'I'm scared that sirens will blast and water will stream from jets in the ceiling.'

'Don't panic,' he said. 'We have a cleaner.'

'Oh, do *we* now?' she asked, pulling a la-di-dah face at Kane. Kane grinned back at her, all too-big teeth and goofy dependence, and her stomach flutters coagulated back into that odd sensation of longing.

'His name is Matt,' Kane explained. 'He

comes in most days and vacuums and gardens and turns on the dishwasher.'

'The dishwasher?' she repeated, sneaking a look at James. 'My, oh, my. Whatever would *we* do without him?'

She was surprised to find that the engaging half-smile had not left James's face. She looked determinedly away.

'And he picks me up from school,' Kane continued, oblivious to the undercurrents swirling about the small room. 'And he stays on sometimes when Dad has a job to finish or has to go out to see clients.'

'I see,' she said, though she clearly didn't. The image of tousled blonde hair came to mind and she wondered briefly what the sunshiny, piano-top woman in their lives did when James had to finish a 'job' or see clients.

But that hardly mattered. She was feeling decidedly better about being in the house of teenage hell than she would ever have expected—and there was no point in pushing her luck.

She picked up a cotton swab.

'Ouch!' Kane was already wincing before the swab was within a foot of his elbow.

'You are making me feel mean, Kane!'

'Matt did a first aid course because he used to be an ambulance driver,' Kane, said, his eyes growing huge. 'Why did you?'

'I am a Cabin Director with MaxAir—you know the airline with the light blue planes? And I have to look after any people who become unwell whilst flying, so I do an extensive first aid course every year. Did you know that way back in the beginning, the first ever flight attendants were actually nurses?'

Obviously Kane was not nearly as impressed with her qualifications as he was with Matt's so she decided on another tack. 'If it makes you feel any better, I have taken a zillion other courses too.'

'Like what sort?'

'I have taken lessons on fixing leaking taps, self-defence, I have a scuba licence and I can speak four languages.'

'Four?' Kane asked, his pale brown eyes growing large.

'Yep. My parents were both born in Italy so I knew Italian before I knew English, but I can also speak conversational German and French.' *I can also juggle, even soft drink cans, which would have sent Jessica into a fit had she been told; I can do the splits and tango with the best of them,* she thought, feeling a bit like a circus clown.

Kane's eyes all but popped out of his head.

'Would you like me to teach you how to say one to ten in Italian?' she asked.

Kane nodded.

'Excellent. Okay. *Uno*…' Siena dabbed at the scrape with the soaked cotton wool, wiping away specks of dried blood and gravel and doing her dandiest to keep Kane's eyes on her mouth as she spoke, not on her hands as she tended his stinging wound.

'*Due*…' Siena cleaned the scrape and patted it dry.

'*Tre*…' Siena unwound the child-proof lid of the top of the antiseptic bottle.

'*Quattro*…' Siena tipped a healthy amount of antiseptic on to a fresh hunk of cotton wool.

'*Cinque*…' Siena dabbed at the scrape, turning Kane's arm a dull brown.

'*Sei*…' Siena put the lid back on to the bottle.

'*Sette*…' Siena tore a hunk of bandage.

'*Otto*…' Siena placed the bandage over Kane's arm.

'*Nove*…' Siena ran a soft hand over the bandage, making sure it was in place.

'*Dieci*! Well done! To the both of us. Now, can you remember them all?'

He shook his head. 'Tell me again.'

Siena did so and had Kane repeat after her. Halfway through she felt a tingle on the back of her neck and she realised it was because James was watching her still. She glanced at him sideways. His half-smile had graduated into something not bigger but *warmer* and she felt a ridiculous flash of satisfaction.

A few moments later Siena realised she was still staring, caught up in James's complex gaze for so long that she now knew he had a ring of midnight-blue around his silvery pupils.

James swallowed, his Adam's apple bobbing

in his strong throat, and Siena had the distinct feeling he would have been able to describe the exact colour of her eyes too.

'Teach me another language!' Kane insisted, shattering the extraordinary tension that had cocooned the room.

'Not now,' James said, as he took Kane by the hand and drew him off the seat. 'I, for one, am in need of a drink.'

And, by the gravel echoing in his voice, Siena had the feeling that if it were not for the presence of Kane, a gin and tonic would have suited him better than lemonade too.

'Can I tempt you?' he asked.

She stood, shoving her hands into the back pockets of her jeans. She knew he was talking about something as innocent as lemonade, but the implications of what it could have meant in a parallel universe resonated through her.

'With lemonade?' she qualified. 'You bet.'

'Yippee,' Kane said. 'Then I can show you my bedroom.'

And, just like that, Siena's breath was sapped from her lungs.

CHAPTER THREE

'Um, I don't know, Kane…' Siena said, backing away physically and mentally.

Before she could duck out the door Kane reached out and grabbed her hand, small, hot, sticky fingers closing over hers. 'But I just got a new computer and it plays games and songs and stuff.'

His pale brown eyes began to glisten. His bottom lip trembled. A screaming kid she could handle. She'd been a pretty competent screaming kid once herself. But a kid with big brown eyes welling with tears? First she'd felt empathy for Freddy the cola-flinger and now this? It seemed that, despite the protestations of some of her cabin crew, she was only human after all.

'You know what,' Siena said, backtracking frantically, 'I would love to see your backyard more. The reason I was driving down this street in the first place was because when I was your age I used to live in this very house.'

'You did?' Kane asked, his expression now wary.

'I did. And the backyard was my favourite place. We had a swing set and a pool, and there was this one fence paling that was never attached properly and when I was not much bigger than you I could slip right through the hole it made.'

'I know! Dad fixed it though when we first moved in. Wow, how cool. Which room was yours?'

'The front room, I'd hazard to guess,' James said.

Siena turned to him and nodded. 'How'd you guess?'

'When we repainted it took me a week to plug up all the holes left by poster pins.'

She grinned. 'I was madly in love with several grunge rock bands for quite some time and I proved my love by covering every spare inch of pink floral wallpaper.'

'I've no doubt,' he said, the half-smile drawing her in. 'And now?'

'My tastes have become more…grown-up.'

'R and B?'

'No. Reality,' she said.

He laughed, the sound rolling over her like an ocean wave on the hottest day of summer, and Siena felt herself warming from the inside out. Okay, now she recognised what this feeling was. It was the zing that came from flirting, and flirting well.

But there was a kid, and a blonde, and crucial dry cleaning to consider. She determinedly switched conversational tack. 'My brother Rick sold this place about three years ago. Rick Capuletti. Did you buy it from him?'

'Dad bought this house for Mum as a wedding present,' Kane all but shouted, delighted to be able to nudge his way back into the conversation.

Her gaze switched straight from Kane to James to find herself drowning in the suddenly unfathomable depths behind his cool grey eyes. Before her eyes his clear-cut edges blurred, the sharpness that had earlier seduced her into easy flirtation dissolving until Siena had to fight the urge to reach out and tug him back to the present.

'Oh,' she said, unable to dredge up a trace of eloquence. *Oh, indeed.* So the sunshiny blonde was not just a ring-in. She was a bona fide Dillon family member. And she was Kane's mother. And, of all things, she had been given a rather pricey *house* as a wedding present.

Wait a second...

'But we only sold this place—' Too late she shut her trap. *Three years ago*, she had been about to say. But the implication was there all the same. Kane had not been a honeymoon baby. Suddenly it was obvious that he had come from the same gene pool as the brown-eyed woman in the photograph, but it was entirely possible that Kane was not James's natural born kid.

James's cheek twitched and she knew he was following the trail of her thoughts without any trouble. She felt herself burning up. Blushing. She! Forthright, tough as nails, unflappable she.

James stood, drawing Kane in front of him as a wall. Kane took the attention blindly, hugging on to his dad's arms as he blinked ingenuously up at Siena.

'Kane, how about you show Siena your new trampoline while I organise the lemonade?'

'Sounds like a plan,' she said, torn halfway between mortification for somehow upsetting her host and a more selfish gratitude that a tour of the upstairs bedrooms had gone by the wayside.

Kane tugged her hand again and they jogged together through the kitchen, leaving James setting some glasses and a plate of packet biscuits on to a tray.

'First I'll show you Dad's shed,' Kane said, taking her to a large rendered concrete outbuilding, which was a new addition to the beautifully manicured backyard. She barely had time to take in the elegant landscaping around their old kidney-shaped in-ground pool as Kane gave the shed's heavy side door a big heave-ho.

And inside?

Inside was a cave of wonders.

Sunlight streamed in through high windows, collecting waves of flying wood dust as it settled upon sharp, clean, oil-soaked tools residing in neat rows along the far wall. A long oak work table was clear of debris and bric-a-brac but was coated with splotches of paint and notches from slipped tools. A sander and a set of clear plastic goggles lay strewn on the bench as though forgotten in the middle of a job. Chunks of wood and chopped tree trunks with the bark still attached lay in neat piles all along the left wall.

'What does your dad do out here?' Siena asked, her voice a little breathless.

'He makes cabinets.' Kane swished his hand like a model on a game show displaying white goods.

She ran her hand along the bench, the soft pads of her fingers tingling at the feel of the rough worn wood. When she reached the end of the bench she found something large hiding beneath a dusty old sheet. She barely hesitated before giving the cloth a tug.

A small gasp escaped her lips as it fell away

to reveal the most beautiful piece of furniture she had ever seen.

It was a baby's changing table—waist-high, with five drawers, resting on stubby little legs. The name *Lachlan* was carved in a heavy neat scrawl along the top drawer and pictures of teddy bears and rattles were carved randomly about the piece.

The detail and craftsmanship was spectacular. In amongst the thousand and one classes she had crammed into her days off, she had taken wood shop. She had lovingly created what she had thought to be a truly beautiful wooden ashtray, though nobody she knew smoked. It had taken days to carve the simple round shape, buff it to a polish and then carve her initials into the bottom.

But this was a whole other dimension. Each piece of wood was obviously chosen for its peculiar grain, with the graded waves of colour and knots working to form a beautiful inclusive whole.

It was exquisite. The work of someone with patience and imagination. Siena had thought

James Dillon a simple labourer, but for once her first impression had been wrong. The man was a creator.

She looked over her shoulder and through the large window which gave an unimpeded view of the backyard and the rear of the two-storey house.

The man in question ambled past the kitchen window with the phone to his ear—calling for a tow truck? Calling for a cab to take her home?

Her heart slipped in her chest and she felt something akin to loss at the thought of leaving so soon. A hand fluttered to her ribs and she swallowed hard. *That* sensation was the most unexpected of all.

She stepped back, needing to distance herself from all of the unwelcome feelings tumbling inside her and she bumped into a small work desk in the corner. A battered, dust-covered laptop resting on the corner of the desk slipped and she turned and caught it before it fell.

She righted it upon its small metal desk and saw that it was loaded on to a simple black webpage with a neat cream font. She knew by the format that it was a web-based diary—a blog. She'd trawled online blogs often as many of her workmates used them to keep their families apprised of their adventures travelling.

This page was simply called 'DINAH' and the dates below the title told Siena it was dedicated to a woman who had died a little over twelve months before. Cold fingers of dread crept up the back of her neck.

Needing to know, to make sure that what she was thinking was true, she ran her finger over the mouse pad to shuffle down the webpage and she randomly chose an entry dated a few months before.

I've been feeling a little anxious over the past few days. I can't put my finger on the reason why, but part of it involves Kane complaining off and on about not feeling well.

Siena looked over her shoulder. Kane was busy in the corner, babbling away about how he helped his dad every Saturday morning and his dad let him choose the sandpaper and that he made five dollars a day when he worked with him. But it soon became white noise as Siena ached to read more. To know more.

She licked her dry lips, her heart suddenly beating so hard she could hear it thrumming in her ears.

But wasn't this like reading the guy's diary? Well, no. By definition a blog was *out there*, on the World Wide Web for all and sundry to stumble upon and read.

Convinced enough, she read on.

Sometimes it is a stomach ache, sometimes a sore throat, sometimes a headache.

I know that this can be a symptom that his counsellors are looking for to say he needs more intensive therapy, but it's winter and a lot of colds are still going around so maybe I am overreacting.

To tell you the truth, I think I know how he feels.

Having moved my business to my back-

yard after they convinced me it would be in Kane's best interests, having cut down time spent with friends and colleagues so that Kane can have every ounce of attention I can give, I have come to a point where there are days when I don't see the point in getting up early or showering, I don't want to eat breakfast, much less make it for someone else, and the thought of going outside the front door leaves me in a cold sweat.

But then I think of that sad little face, of those big brown eyes, so like his mother's, and of that one important day a year ago when he asked me ever so politely not go to work so far away again, and my love for him takes over.

For him I can and will do anything.

One step at a time.

Siena blinked.

Dinah. Dinah was the beautiful blonde with the bedroom eyes in the photograph on the piano. Dinah was Kane's mother, the woman who had been given a whole house as a wedding gift. And she was gone.

'Hey, do you want to see *my* swings? They're way better than the ones you left behind.'

Siena spun around to find Kane standing at her back, staring at her with big brown eyes full of innocence. If she thought her heart was thrumming earlier she'd had no idea. She could feel it slamming against her chest. Her palms were sweating. Her face had turned beet-red with guilt.

What was she thinking in reading James's blog? Was she insane? Obviously the humidity was sending her barmy.

'Sure, Kane,' she said, spinning him on the spot and giving him a little shove towards the door with one hand as she closed the laptop behind her with the other. 'But we'll have to be quick as it's time for me to go.'

James hung up the phone from calling a tow-truck.

He leant his palms against the kitchen bench

and watched his son dragging Siena out of his workshop and over to the trampoline.

She padded behind him on bare feet, her heavy dark curls bouncing, the hem of her long jeans dragging in the dirt, but she seemed not to notice or care.

Kane clambered up on to his new toy and she stood by, hands on hips, as Kane bounced up and down and chatted away about goodness knew what.

James breathed in deep through his nose.

Siena Capuletti was something else, and, no matter which way he looked at it, they had been engaged in some pretty darned enjoyable flirting back in the bathroom. He didn't even really know whether he had started it or her, but before he'd even known what he was doing he'd found himself in one heck of a natural rhythm.

He rolled the kinks out of his shoulders, quite liking the feeling that he had stretched some muscles that hadn't been stretched in a good long time.

He didn't have time to think on it much more

as suddenly Siena was jogging back through the kitchen door.

'I can't believe how thirsty I am,' she said as she leaned against the kitchen bench at his side. 'It's so hot out there. But, then again, it's hot out there every day here.' She glanced pointedly at the tray of drinks which had never gone further than the kitchen. 'May I?'

James nodded, watching her drink the tall glass of soft drink in one go, as if she stopped she might not get started again.

As she drank she reached up and rubbed a hand across the back of her neck, ruffling the curls spread along her neckline, and it occurred to James for the first time that she herself might have been injured in the accident.

He frowned. Once he'd known Kane was all right that should have been the first thing he'd ascertained. What was with him these days? So what if he could spin a line or two; he obviously didn't seem to know how to think logically any more. Had he spent so much time watching over Kane that he had forgotten how to speak to an adult? Lemonade and cookies? Come on!

Siena continued running her fingers up through the back of her curls until they tumbled back against her neck in messy disarray. Okay, so she didn't seem hurt. She just seemed to like to run her hands through her hair. He didn't blame her. The affect of those bouncing dark curls agreed with him plenty.

'Pretty nifty set-up you have out there,' she said, when she came up for breath. She licked a sheen of lemonade from her lips. 'I kind of peeked a look at the changing table you were working on. It's gorgeous. Really. You're very talented.'

He tipped his head in thanks. 'So they tell me.'

'What would one have to fork out for one of those?' she asked.

She leant a hip against his bench and crossed her feet at the ankle, revealing a truly dirty underneath of her right foot.

He glanced at the floor to see a run of dirty footprints. He bit his lip, thinking Matt would have a fit when he found them marking the white kitchen floor.

But to James they kind of felt like the first footsteps on the moon. They were proof of a proper grown-up conversation he was having in his kitchen, which was something unique and a bit of a breakthrough really.

'You'd have to pay more than you would think,' he admitted. 'That one is actually commissioned for the forthcoming son of a ridiculously prominent Aussie actor, which I'm sure would never have happened if my pieces didn't cost so much.'

'Is that a polite way of telling me I couldn't afford one?'

'Not at all,' he said, his throat tickled by bubbles of laughter. 'Though you would have to get in line.'

She lifted one eloquent eyebrow in a very convincing show of antipathy. But, rather than putting him in his place, it only made him realise that he liked that dextrous eyebrow of hers almost as much as he liked those disorderly curls.

'Since I began working from home I'm embarrassed to admit that the Dillon label has taken off exponentially by way of its sudden scarcity,' he said, leaning his own hip against the bench, mirroring her stance. 'My business manager is in heaven as it has meant he can put prices on each piece which, since I am rarely at the showroom, I cannot veto.'

'Okay,' she said, holding up a hand like a traffic cop. 'I get it. I probably couldn't afford one!'

Again he laughed, and again he revelled in the feeling of using his lungs for more than just taking in oxygen for the first time in all too long.

'But doesn't being home all the time drive you nuts?'

'Nope. I can work my own hours and there's a permanently open intercom in the wall in case Kane needs me. I wouldn't want to be anywhere else.'

He didn't go so far as to admit that in the last few months his life had so come to revolve around Kane's moods that he was pretty certain he could have turned the intercom off and known if and when Kane was distressed anyway. Even *he* knew that would put a damper on the whole chatting to a regular girl like he was a regular guy thing he had going on.

'Yeah, I don't know,' she said, her two front teeth nipping uncertainly at her lower lip. 'I wonder if I was staring at the same four walls all the time I might not go a little batty.'

'Don't the insides of your planes begin to look alike?' he asked.

She seemed to think about it for a second before she said, 'Nah. Not when you add two hundred new faces per plane to the mix.'

'Fair point. So how long have you been flying high?' he asked, suddenly needing to prolong this thing, this feeling, this whatever it was that was making him feel so loose as long as he could.

But he soon cringed as her right eyebrow flickered and threatened to shoot skyward. It had been so long since he'd had to ingratiate himself to someone new he was obviously pretty rusty. Had he said something wrong? Had it sounded like some sort of chat-up line? But he wasn't trying to chat her up. He was just chatting.

She blinked up at him, her mouth twisting as she warily weighed his words. 'Seven years,' she said. 'Why?'

'I've never met a live one in the real world before. I had kind of reached the conclusion you guys were all well-trained robots kept in some warehouse up Max's Port Douglas head-quarters,' he said before he had even tried the words out in his head.

Note to self—think before you talk.

Siena looked down at her bare feet, her shaggy curls flicking over her head. 'Do *I* look like a robot?'

'Oh, no. You seem plenty real to me,' he said. And, okay, that time he meant every ounce of flirtation wholeheartedly. How could he not? It felt so darned good.

When she looked back up James was awarded a lopsided smile brimming with appreciation for his efforts and somewhere deep down inside him something shifted. Big time. Not at all prepared for such a shift, he tried to shift it back. But it was too late.

As James struggled internally, her eyes

narrowed as though she was trying to figure him out. Or perhaps she was just trying to place him. Maybe they *did* know one another. Maybe that was all this shifting sensation was. Not attraction but familiarity. He was about to ask if they had met before, but even he knew that would absolutely sound like a line.

'Firstly,' she said, spare hand now firmly on her jutted out hip, 'I am not just any old *flight attendant*. I am one of the top Cabin Directors on MaxAir's international corridor. And secondly, the only reason I am in this get-up, rather than my favourite Dolce suit, pristine make-up, without a wind-up key sticking out of my back, thank-you very much, is because some kid spilt cola all over me on the plane up here from Melbourne. Please tell me Kane-o doesn't drink cola.'

Kane-o? What was this woman on? Whatever it was he wanted some.

'He doesn't drink cola,' James repeated like a good little acolyte, eternally grateful he had thought before saying that *last* gem out loud. 'Matt showed Kane the cola and coin trick and

Kane is now petrified of the stuff. He's more scared of cola than he is of the dark.'

As he had really hoped they would, her bow mouth kicked up at the corner and her ocean-green eyes sparkled. Damn it, but she was lovely.

'Excellent,' she said, nodding so hard her curls bounced about her ears before settling in messy disarray, framing her flushed cheeks.

'Excellent,' James repeated, his voice sounding heavy and languid in the hot air. Was the air hot? The air-conditioning was on but it sure felt hot.

The room went quiet as the two of them ran out of things to say. James searched for a conversation topic but he could find nothing. His mind was too full with the warring tangle of magnetism and self-reproach for daring to go there in the first place.

'So, is the tow-truck on its way?' Siena asked, setting the glass on the sink with such care he wondered if she had read his mind. She tugged on her ear. 'You were on the phone a minute ago.'

'It's on its way.'

Siena felt awash with relief at the news. She didn't want to have to call Rufus, Max's complimentary driver, charming, chatty and playful as he was. Not. But it was time to go.

Mostly because after accidentally reading James's blog she now knew why those cool grey flecks shrouded his once happy eyes. And, rather than making her feel further estranged from his situation, she felt…moved. Moved enough to stay cooped up in his suburban kitchen trading wisecracks when she should have been busy getting on with her day. The truth was she itched to see what would happen if that half-smile of his morphed into the real thing.

But that didn't matter, because in two days she *would* be on a plane back to Melbourne—either to bury herself in the employment section of the newspaper or, if she was able to convince Max of it, packing her bags for a move to Rome—the furthest place from Cairns she could imagine.

It suddenly occurred to her that she was mirroring James's stance exactly, or he was mirroring hers, casually leaning against the kitchen bench, hands leaning inches apart along the sink's edge, knees pointed to one another. Yep, it was way past time for her to go.

'Excellent,' she said again, clapping her hands together nice and loud to break through the loaded silence. 'I'll wait outside. Must make sure they take the car where I want it to go lest my brother kill me.'

She backed away towards the front door, thinking that might be goodbye, but James followed, watching her with those dark, sombre, but really quite lovely eyes of his. She again felt the atypical thread of longing and attraction tugging her through the midriff.

Uh-uh. Nope. No way…

She skipped over to the piano, grabbed her tipped-over handbag and then made a beeline for the front door.

In her haste she tripped backwards over a rug at the front door. James reached out and grabbed her by the wrist, pulling her upright until they stood nose to nose.

While her balance steadied her breathing

pace rocketed away. James's workman's grip was strong. Her wrist burned from his touch. She caught a waft of wood shavings and cedar oil. The guy smelled of tradition and family and home.

A flash of memory caught her off-guard. Her dad used to insist the dining table remain polished to a high shine. She'd always had the feeling her mother had liked it that way and he had continued the tradition after she was gone. It had been one chore she hadn't minded, the smell of cedar so delicious, the act of running oil over a smooth surface calming, productive, helpful, always eliciting a pat on the head from her dad when the deed was done…

The memory, the scent, the house, him—it was all so heady she felt herself swaying.

James's grip tightened, his other hand reaching around to rest lightly at her waist. But, rather than adding to her confusion, his gallantry only honed her focus. She didn't need some guy to save her when she fell. She had picked herself up enough times to know she could do it fine on her own.

'Thanks,' she said, her voice a giveaway throaty whisper.

She twisted her hand from his grasp, spun about on now sturdy legs and bounded out the door, grabbing her shoes as she shot past but not stopping to put them on.

As the green monster came into view her footsteps slowed as she saw how badly she had messed up. The whole bonnet was crushed and twisted. The smell of burnt oil scorched the air. Surely it was a write-off.

Insurance was the least of her problems. With the money from the sale of the house she could afford to fix it, or buy ten new ones. The problem was Rick. He'd spent a lifetime calling her irresponsible, antagonistic, the type to shoot first and ask questions later, and within half an hour of being home she had rashly taken a drive straight to the one place she had so purposefully avoided all these years. She had gone and proved him right.

As she neared the car she realised the damage went further. Before she had hit the tree, the beast's tyres had trampled one of a group of small rose bushes. Siena had planted those rose bushes with her father on a warm spring day. She remembered his crinkling hazel eyes smiling down at her as though she was his little princess. The memories crowding her were too much.

'Oh, I am so sorry,' she whispered, her sudden sorrow deeper than concern for a couple of squished roses.

'Don't worry about it,' James said from right behind her.

She flinched as his nearness drew her from her reverie. Cedar oil, family, home…

'Truly,' she said, turning to him, but backing away in the same move, choosing to believe the apology had been for him alone. 'I took an advanced gardening class a couple of summers ago. You'll be able to replant the bush, if that is any consolation.'

She didn't offer to do so. Offering to clean up Kane's wound had only created more problems than it had fixed.

James crouched down and pulled a perfect rose from under the tyre. Its stem was squished at the base but the flower was unblemished. An iceberg rose. Cool. White. Perfect.

'Here,' he said. 'You liberated it; you may as well take it.' He held out the flower, tipping its beautiful head towards her so that she caught a whiff of the soft perfume.

Siena baulked, the gesture so intimate and inadvertently romantic she had no idea what to do.

She saw the moment that James hesitated too. His eyes zeroed in on the rose, then back to her again, the cool grey depths burning with some unknown memory.

Had she hurt his feelings by not simply taking the damn thing? Was he remembering a similar moment with his wife? Either way, she couldn't handle seeing the ache behind his eyes as she couldn't dampen down the mirrored ache it created in her.

She planted a big wide grin upon her face, then reached out and snatched it from his hand.

'Thanks, James. I was the one who plucked it, of sorts, so it is rightfully mine.' She held the velvet-soft petals to her nose and sniffed. 'Mmm. Gorgeous.'

At that moment a small red hatchback turned into James's driveway and pulled to a halt. James leapt back from her as though he only then realised he had been standing on a bed of hot coals.

A lanky fiftyish guy with long grey hair tied back in a ponytail unfolded himself from the tight front seat. His eyes twinkled and a huge lopsided grin creased his craggy face.

'Morning, dude!' he said, loping up to James and slapping him on the back.

James rocked stiffly on to his toes and back on to heavy flat feet. His lips thinned and he couldn't look the newcomer in the eye. 'Hey, Matt. Kane's on the trampoline if you want to say hello.'

Matt's bushy grey eyebrows rose. 'On a school day? Again?'

It hadn't even occurred to Siena that it was a school day. It was…Thursday? She never had any idea what day it was. Her roster was always different, rotating three days on, two days off. Unlike the time in her life when things like school and weekends and bedtimes had mattered, the *day* no longer meant a thing.

But to a guy with a school-aged son…?

'He wasn't feeling well,' James said.

Stomach aches, sore throat, headaches— Siena remembered all too clearly from James's blog.

'Well, naturally that's why the trampoline would hold so much attraction for him,' Matt said under his breath before turning a sudden, beaming, unevenly toothed smile in her direction. 'Now, who might this lovely young flower be?'

He glanced at the rose twirling in her hand, then looked from Siena to James and Siena again with a big goofy grin on his face. If he had reached out and nudged James with his elbow she would not have been surprised.

I almost ran over his kid with my car! she wanted to scream, loathing the fact that she wasn't the only one thinking that there was something curious happening between her and the man looking resolutely anywhere but at her.

'Siena Capuletti,' she said, saving James the trouble. 'Driver of the big green monster wrapped around James's tree, at your service.'

She held out a hand and Matt gave it a hearty shake.

'Siena used to live in this house when she was younger,' James added, finding his voice again.

'Well, I am sure pleased to meet you, Siena. Any relation to Rick Capuletti? The mechanic in town?'

'He's my brother,' she admitted.

'Right on! Tell him O'Connor said hi.'

'Shall do,' Siena promised, though she had a feeling that Rick wouldn't hear much through the steam pouring from his ears.

She was saved from further scrutiny by the longed-for arrival of the tow-truck.

'Hey, this is Rick's car,' the large hairy driver shouted as he slid from his high cab, paunch first.

'Rick's sister,' Siena said with a sigh, pointing to her chest.

'Oh, right. The deserter,' the tow-truck driver said.

Yep. That sounded like Rick—able to grate on her nerves even through a third party.

She should have known she couldn't slip away quietly in the twilight after all this. Even though Cairns was practically a city hub now compared with when she had left, everyone still knew everyone. Everyone would know she was in town, everyone would know she had crashed her brother's car, and now everyone would know that she had spent part of her day with James Dillon—widower.

'The car's unlocked, so how about we get her all hooked up and outta here before word gets back to my two hundred pound brother with a temper to match?' she said, using her polite but insistent sky girl voice.

She clicked her fingers and the driver remembered who he was—a guy who got paid by the number of jobs he delivered in a day. That put a spring in his step as he hotfooted back to the winch.

She turned to Matt and James, who were watching the interplay, and she felt she owed it to them to tell them who the Capulettis were.

'I grew up here,' she explained. 'I moved away several years ago and this is my first time back and my big brother is a pain in the butt who should mind his own business.'

It was such an impressive introduction she felt she ought to curtsy at the end.

'Families, eh?' Matt said. 'You can't live with 'em.'

Siena grinned. 'That's the bumper sticker of my life.'

'So you don't live around here any more?' James asked, honing in on the essentials.

'No,' she said, shaking her head and concentrating on the rose rather than on the setback in James's eyes. 'Melbourne. Mainly.'

'Melbourne,' Matt repeated, his face screwing up as if he had sucked on a lemon. 'Why would anyone move to cold rainy Melbourne after knowing about this slice of heaven?'

'Oh, I don't know,' she shot back. 'Maybe the world class sport, fantastic restaurants, out of this world shopping, the art and culture and actual seasons might be considered a drawcard to some.'

'Shopping?' Matt repeated. 'Well, now I'm convinced.'

James made a sound that sounded a heck of a lot like a snort of laughter. Her gaze skittered to his, to find his eyes sparkling.

The sparkle hinted at the warmth she had felt in his fingers when he had gripped her arm earlier. The warmth reminded her of what the guy looked like when he smiled. The memory of that smile made Siena feel as if she was once again enclosed in this single dad's unwitting gravitational pull. And *that* reminded her why she wanted to leave his presence as soon as was humanly possible.

She dragged her eyes away from his, gave a brief goodbye glance at the old house, a demon she had quite proudly slaughtered that day for sure, then with a quick wave goodbye jogged over to the truck, and asked to bum a ride with the driver.

'I can watch Kane if you need James to give you a lift somewhere,' Matt called out, giving James a bump with his shoulder at the same time.

'No, thanks,' she said, giving them both a big wave as she leapt into the cab and mentally hurried the tow-truck driver, who was taking way too much time winching the green monster on to his truck. Funny, but she instinctively knew it would be easier to suffer Rick's temper than share a confined space with James Dillon.

'I'd better be there when this arrives or Rick will blow a gasket,' she called out. 'Thanks for the lemonade, though. And thank Kane for the tour of your workshop. It really was a delight.'

The driver hauled his bulky frame into the high cab and she could have kissed him, though he was much further down the evolutionary scale than the types of guys she usually saw than even James.

'Ready to go?' he asked.

'You bet.' *More than you know*, she thought, for although Siena was experiencing stomach flutters of the first order, she was free as a bird and the Dillon house was already a cage to the men who lived there.

Matt gave her one last wave before heading indoors.

James wasn't so easily swayed.

As the tow-truck diver pulled away, she watched James in the side mirror all the way to the corner. Standing there in his tired jeans and his dusty T-shirt, with his lean muscled arms hanging loosely at his sides, he didn't move.

As she travelled down the long, gently winding road, he stood on the footpath, beside his squished roses, watching her go.

CHAPTER FOUR

'So are you sticking with this airline gig?' Rick asked when they were alone in the kitchen after an early dinner that night. 'Or have you come to Cairns to give Max the flick?'

Siena sat back at the kitchen bench nibbling on a fingernail and flicking through a pile of junk mail while the twins ran out the last of their energy, Tina put baby Rosie to bed and Rick put the leftovers into freezer bowls.

'Of course I'm sticking with it,' she said, her feet jiggling as they rested on a bar at the bottom of her stool. 'Why wouldn't I be?'

'You always did get bored pretty quick.' His thick dark eyebrows shifted skyward, willing her to argue as she distractedly flicked through the pages of some magazine. She slammed the magazine shut and sat on her hands.

'I have a low attention span. It's not just me; it's the bane of my generation. You wouldn't know about that being that you are *so* much older.' She shot Rick a bratty smile and he scowled back.

'When *did* you go so grey, *Riccione?*' she asked, throwing his proper name in his face, her diabolical inner teenager taking over.

'It appeared overnight the day after you ran away,' Rick said, his terrorising older brother mechanism kicking in as though it hadn't been dormant for seven years.

Deep breaths, she thought. *Happy place…*

'I think you actually care about this job, sis.'

She knew by the look in his eye that Rick was thinking it was because some of his *guidance* when she was younger may have rubbed off. Rubbed the wrong way, more like.

'Unbelievably, my wayward little sister cares for something other than the wind at her back.'

'What, me? Care?' she said, holding a hand to her heart. 'Never!' But care she did. She really didn't want to have to tell Max no.

'So now we've exhausted work, how are

things on the boyfriend front?' he asked. 'In cousin Ash's last email he mentioned you had a fellow in New York the last time you visited him on a layover. But the last I heard you were hot and heavy with some guy in Paris.'

She watched him closely to see if he was sending her a sideways barb that the two of them hadn't communicated by phone or email for months. But his question seemed genuine. She bit down the thought that it was her own guilt for not keeping in touch that was niggling at her.

'Not a *fellow* as such,' she said. 'Gage and I share an obsession for home-made gnocchi and he knows exactly where to find the best Italian in New York. And with Raoul in Paris it's all about good coffee. I have discovered I have a knack for cultivating casual friendships made in heaven.'

Something crashed in the next room followed by a slowly increasing wail of a twin who had done something wrong. Rick threw a tea towel over his shoulder and went to find out what was going on. But at the doorway he stopped and turned.

'There is one problem with having a guy in every port, *Piccolo.*'

Siena's chin raised an inch. 'What's that?' she asked, knowing she couldn't stop him from telling her anyway.

'There comes a time when there's no safe place left to run but home.'

Rick pushed his way through the swing doors and Siena was left alone with nothing to do with her clenched fists but unclench them.

Siena's mobile phone buzzed, giving her an outlet. She waited for a name to appear on her screen but it was an unfamiliar mobile number.

Rufus? Maximillian?

She answered the phone. 'Hello?'

'Siena?'

James. She hardly knew the guy but his name popped into her mind the second his deep, well-modulated voice said her name.

'It's James. James Dillon from this afternoon.'

No kidding, she thought, but all she said was, 'Hello again.'

'Um, you left your PDA at my place. I found it on the piano when it started beeping madly about fifteen minutes ago and I wasn't sure how to get it to stop, so I pressed lots of buttons until it did.'

Beeping? Oh, right, it would be a reminder that her next week's flight schedule would have appeared in her email inbox—

'Then I figured it was beeping for a reason,' he continued, 'so you might want it back ASAP. The only way to find you was to go looking until I found Rick's address and your mobile number… Anyway, I'm at the lights on the corner of Henderson Street right now and I'll be there in about thirty seconds.'

Siena leapt from the kitchen stool. 'Oh, right. Okay.'

The last thing she wanted at that moment was handsome James Dillon knocking at Rick's front door. Especially right after his charming 'guy in every port' comment.

Especially since, after the tow-truck had dropped her and the smashed Ute at Rick's Body Shop, she'd stayed there pondering the idea quite extensively that if James had the same lifestyle and fly-by-night personality as New York Gage, or even bold Raoul in Paris, he would have been serious casual friendship material.

Heck, the second she had laid eyes on him, half the cells in her body had rocketed to life. The connection she had felt to him had been electric. But, within the same second, once it had sunk in that he was Kane's father, every other cell had already begun to resist everything he had to offer.

'I'll meet you out front,' she offered, her mind turning with ways to get past Rick and out the front door. Boy, if the world wasn't spinning to make her feel like a sixteen-year-old all over again! 'Rick's place is the one with the nauseating Triton fountain in the front yard.'

'Thanks. See you soon.' And then he hung up.

Siena pressed the phone off, listened carefully to see where Rick was, then just gave in and made a run for it down the hall and out the front door. The change of air from air-conditioned cool to hot and humid made her skin clammy in half a second.

She power-walked down the gravel driveway as a sleek, dark sedan pulled up by Rick's letterbox. The tinted window rolled down and Siena jogged up to meet its inhabitant.

'I've got your package,' James said out of the corner of his mouth like some sort of Chicago gangster. Some breathtakingly handsome gangster made up of shadows and clean-cut lines who made her heart beat faster in her chest. Although that could have been the escape from Alcatraz that had her adrenalin in high gear.

He waved her PDA at her with one long-fingered hand. Long fingers with short finger-nails. Tanned knuckles covered in a fine spray of ash-brown hair. Not smooth and manicured like the guys she usually made friends with.

James Dillon had a real man's hands. And she really *really* liked them. And his inadvertently sexy two-day-old stubble. And his woodsy scent...

'What'll it cost me?' Siena asked, crouching down and resting her palms on her knees.

He leaned out the window, resting his tanned forearm along the window frame until his face was lit by moonlight. 'Thanks and a smile from a pretty lady are all this chump will ever need.'

Even though the air was so humid she could feel it slithering over every inch of bare skin, her throat went dry. He handed her the PDA. 'Thanks,' she said, and though she tried to smile she found that for this guy she couldn't fake it.

'No worries.'

'So where's Kane?' she asked, wondering why she was prolonging this when she should have run inside the minute she had her goods.

'Home with Matt. Helping make dinner. I'm almost too scared to go home to see what I'm in for.'

'Right.'

She nodded. He half-smiled. And, though she knew she ought to give him a friendly salute and run back inside before Rick came looking for her, Siena could feel that same tenuous thread from earlier wrapping itself tighter about her. In darkness and moonlight with the still of night about them it felt stronger still. She feared it might reel her in if she wasn't careful.

She made a move to leave before James spoke up.

'I'm actually glad I had an excuse to come over tonight.'

'You are?' She casually cleared her throat to remove the frog that had surreptitiously made itself at home there.

'I wanted to thank you,' he said. 'It has been a long time since I have seen Kane smile like he did today. You see, Kane recently lost his mother.'

At the word *recently*, her heart squeezed tightly in her chest. She knew from reading James's blog that it had been more than twelve months since Dinah's death, but for the guy before her it must feel as raw as the day it happened.

'I'm so sorry,' she said.

He shrugged off her platitude. No doubt he'd heard a thousand just the same. 'You no doubt figured out by Kane's little outburst that I married his mum when he was around five years old. Thankfully, before Dinah died, we had completed the process of Kane's adoption or he could have ended up in the clutches of his father.'

So she'd been right. James wasn't even Kane's natural father. Oh, help! Siena's heart squeezed so tight she could no longer remember how to breathe.

'A drummer,' James continued as though he had no idea that Siena was fast becoming a juddering mess at his side. 'On the road a great deal. Bad news. I just thought you ought to know. To understand.'

She suddenly wanted to know everything, but not enough to ask. Her natural born inclination to run was far too strong, far too ingrained, far too well-heeled. And, though James Dillon may be some kind of catch, for that reason alone she could *not* think of him as *casual friendship* material.

'These past months have been tough,' he continued as though now the floodgates were open he couldn't stop. 'And tougher on him, I am sure. But with you, at home, for both of us today was unexpectedly…fun.'

He said the word as though he hadn't known

what it meant until that moment. He didn't smile. He didn't even flicker a dimple. But still Siena was moved beyond the capacity she thought possible.

With a deep breath she moved in and placed a hand over his, fighting against the zing that ran up her arm, and said, 'It was fun for me too. Who would have guessed that a scare like the one I gave the lot of us would lead to that? Sometimes it simply takes a change of scene to show you what you are missing.'

It occurred to her that she had seen a million new scenes since the day she'd left home, yet was she really as fulfilled and satisfied with her life as she could have been? The insidious thought took hold and grew roots and again she cursed herself for ever coming back to this town.

She pulled herself together and moved back to a safe distance, her hand sliding over James's fingers and on to the cool of the metal window runner and away.

'Thanks for bringing this back,' she said,

waving her PDA at him as she stepped backwards, further and further away.

'Thanks for the fun. And for listening.'

'Consider us even.'

He watched her leave, his face moving further into the shadows as he slid his arm back into the dark car.

'Goodnight, Siena,' he said.

'Goodbye, James.'

She turned and jogged back along the gravel driveway and into the house without looking back, though she heard the soft sound of his car pulling out on to the road behind her.

She made it into the kitchen just in time for Rick to arrive with one chubby sniffling twin in his arms and the other following behind grinning, both in matching blue denim overalls. If he noticed her pink cheeks and extra humidity-induced curls he didn't say anything.

Siena was all but knocked over by the grinning twin—Leo?—as he bundled up to her, arms raised. 'Auntie 'Enna, up!'

She rested a hand on the kid's head, letting it stay there a moment when she realised how nice the silky soft hair felt between her fingers. Such a cute kid. A cute kid with two loving parents, and as yet no tragedy to temper that cute smile. Nothing yet standing in the way of oodles of future fun…

'Rick, just promise you won't ever tell your kids they're hopeless,' she said out of the blue, shooting first and asking questions later as she always had.

'Excuse me?'

'It might feel like a throwaway line to you, but I promise they won't ever forget it. And, on that note, I'm going to head up to bed. I have a big day tomorrow.'

Rick looked at her so hard, as though if he let her eye contact swerve, she might fly away.

'Right,' he said, drawing his hard eyes from hers to look softly down at his son. 'I think we could all do with a good night's sleep.'

Siena slipped her hand away from Leo's soft head and tucked it in the back of her jeans. 'Great. I'll see you in the morning.'

And then she grabbed her PDA and jogged—no, she ran—up the stairs.

* * *

It was barely eight o'clock when James shut the door to Kane's bedroom, but Kane had been out for the count for fifteen minutes already.

He usually had trouble getting him to sleep as he would fret unless James was in sight right up until he could no longer hold his eyelids open by sheer force of willpower. But that night he'd all but dropped off in the middle of dinner.

Was it really as simple as Siena had suggested—that a change of scene was what Kane needed? Had their routine grown from being a coping mechanism into a stale way of life no longer suitable for either of them? Well, truth be told, the only out of the ordinary thing about that day had been the whirlwind that was Siena Capuletti.

James ran a fast hand over his short hair, trying to shake himself awake by way of follicular stimulation. Now Kane was asleep he had to head back to work.

He walked through his moonlit backyard, grabbing an overturned Tonka truck and Kane's baseball mitt along the way so he could put them away before they were covered in dew.

Once inside his workshop, he pulled the protective sheet off the changing table and stared at it for a full minute. He warmed at the knowledge that Siena had thought his work *gorgeous*. There weren't that many people who could pull off a word like that and get away with it, but coming from her lips it held weight.

He shifted the drop cloth back into place. It was almost done. Who had known that when he had begun to work from home that he would have commissions running into the New Year and beyond? Siena had been right there—*that* change of scene had done his business wonders.

As he dragged up his stool to his work desk, he couldn't help thinking that Siena Capuletti was something a heck of a lot more than right.

A local but not a local.

Kane had repeatedly called her 'cool' as he had run through his crazy afternoon with Matt over dinner. And she *was* cool—those clothes, those shoes, the way she held herself, her natural playfulness.

A 'deserter' the tow-truck driver had called her, which should have been enough to put her a mile from his thoughts—the very *last* thing Kane needed in his life was another tearaway.

But when Matt had called her a 'lovely young flower' he'd exactly put James's feelings into words.

She was simply quite unlike anyone he had ever met—with enough latent energy to light a city. When he had touched her wrist, to catch her when she'd tripped—bam! And again when she had laid her small warm hand over his on the window ledge of his car—the energy had resounded from her fine-boned limb into his hand, shooting sparks up his arm until it had kick-started a deep and all but forgotten pounding in his chest.

That sort of instant attraction was rare— beyond the butterflies a guy couldn't help but feel when noticing a beautiful woman.

Even with Dinah it hadn't been like that. For his part there had been more of a slow burn.

One night on the town, his mob of short-back-and-sides friends had wandered into the hard rock Pig's Head Pub down by the docks wearing their smart casual gear, drinking their pony necked beers, to find a lot of guys saturated in leather and tattoos.

The gang had voted to mosey straight on out of there when they had all seen her—a scrap of a girl with long blonde hair, midriff top, mini-skirt, fishnet tights and heavy black boots, dancing the night away, her eyes closed as though she was shutting out all thought bar the heavy beat of the music.

At the end of the night, James had been sitting alone at the bar, waiting for his mates to come back from the gents, when she had appeared at his side, her blonde hair wild, her skin shiny with sweat, the make-up around her brown bedroom eyes smudged with eyeliner.

'Dinah,' she said, holding out a small hand.

'James,' he returned, shaking her hand. But, rather than warm, which he would have expected after her night of dancing, she felt cold. So very cold. And her small cold hand made him look twice.

'I've been watching you,' she said.

James raised an eyebrow in disbelief. With all the attention she'd had that night he would have thought himself way under the radar.

'Why didn't you ask me to dance?' she asked.

James laughed.

'Finally!' she said, throwing thin arms into the air. 'A smile! I was beginning to wonder if you had the ability.'

James's laughter subsided, but his smile remained. 'I smile plenty when there is something to smile about.'

'Fair enough. Anyway, I'm done here and I would really love to head out of here for a cup of coffee. Are you up for it?'

Are you up for me? she had meant and it had taken James half a second to say yes. From that day they were James and Dinah. The nine-to-five cabinet-maker and the wild child who, it turned out, had a child of her own at home. A shy, gentle three-year-old boy James had fallen in love with at first sight.

He had always wondered in the back of his mind if Dinah had sought him out that night because she was looking for someone safe for her son. But he had loved her anyway, perhaps because of the almost desperate way she needed him.

At her insistence they had moved to the suburbs, at his insistence he had adopted her son, and they had become a car-pooling, dinner party holding, regular family.

Until, at the age of thirty, Dinah had been diagnosed with cirrhosis. After six months of unsuccessful treatment and crying herself to sleep at night blaming herself for her wild youth, she was gone.

But, no matter what he had endured in the last couple of years, it seemed he hadn't been emptied of all aspiration as he had thought. His instincts were whispering just loud enough that he couldn't shout them down.

Siena. Maybe he ought to…what? Ask her on a date while she was in town? Send her flowers? Write her a card? It had been so long since he had done this he wondered if the rules had changed. Did you call a person these days or was it all about sending provocative text messages on one's mobile—?

A noise came through the intercom. His ears pricked up. A shuffling of sheets, a small sniffle, then Kane settled again.

Kane. That one word silenced his whispering instincts in one fell swoop. He had been so busy thinking about what he wanted, what he needed, that he had plumb forgotten about Kane.

James again ran hands through his already over-mussed hair, this time in order to rub away the sudden pounding in his head.

Surely he was messing with forces he had no business messing with. Though Siena was like chalk to Dinah's cheese in many ways, she was young, she lived a four-hour plane flight away and drove in red high heels, for goodness' sake.

And everyone—counsellors, teachers, friends and books and websites alike—all agreed that what Kane needed was time.

His head swimming, James opened his

laptop and found the blank weblog page he was looking for.

The one time *he* had been in such a bad way as to go to counsellors for himself, they had suggested he keep a diary, as though getting his feelings out of his head and down on paper would make it easier to cope.

As a man of the computer age, he had used the blog format instead. Having his words floating out there in the ether made them feel like more of a release than if they were written on paper and tied up in a ribbon at the bottom of his sock drawer, hidden, as though they were a dirty secret.

He cracked his knuckles, freeing up the wave of information he would have to wade through before he could even think about getting to sleep.

And he began to type.

Showered and changed into her favourite red crushed velvet pyjamas—soft, comfortable, easy to pack and a little bit sexy just in case—Siena leant back against a pile of fat frilly floral cushions on the lumpy spare bed and laid her laptop on her thighs as she shuffled her mouse and set to opening her emails.

Despite the PDA's beeping insistence that it ought to be, her schedule wasn't there as yet, which only gave her further heebie-jeebies about what Max had in store for her with his 'fabulous career move'. What else could no schedule mean but no more flights?

There was one email from Parisian Raoul with a subject title so risqué it made her laugh out loud. But it also made Rick's accusation echo in her head. *A guy in every port…* Well, why the heck not? It made her romantic life innocuous and uncomplicated and that was just the way she liked it.

She made a move to open Raoul's email when noises in the hallway drew Siena's gaze to her closed bedroom door. Rick must have been putting the kids to bed. She looked to the clock at the side of her bed to find it was some time after eight.

Her fleeting glance slammed to a halt as she saw the white iceberg rose James had given her lying provocatively on the bedside table.

She reached out and took the rose in her hand, the sweet scent tickling at her nose. It only brought about a strange sense memory of diesel fuel, disinfectant and wood shavings. Who knew such a strange mix of scents could be so evocative?

Before she really knew what she was about to do, Siena ignored Raoul's email and instead typed out a row of letters in the webpage line of her internet browser. She hesitated only a moment before pressing the Enter key.

Within seconds a simple black page loaded on to her screen. And as the word 'DINAH' caught her eye she slammed her laptop shut.

What was she doing? Spying on him? Well, of course she was. But what did it matter? Now she had her PDA back—the PDA which he himself had admitted to snooping through!—she was never going to see the guy again. So how could it hurt to read a very little more?

Slowly, slowly she lifted the screen. There were no photographs on the site. No links. No comment boxes. It was simply the emotional

outpourings of an anonymous guy. Anonymous to anyone who might stumble upon it,
but not to her.

Siena shuffled lower on her bed and picked
out sporadic posts. She read about the home
video collection James had edited together for
Dinah's funeral which he still let Kane watch
in his bedroom on bad nights. She read about
odd floating memories of his time with Dinah's
dysfunctional family, her alcoholic mother and
deadbeat ex, and she understood a little why he
saw himself as Kane's only hope. He revealed
moments when he had felt like giving up, and
worse, the moments when he verbally slapped
himself for even contemplating it.

A good hour later she dragged herself out of
deep tunnel vision when she tasted her own
tears on her lips. But she couldn't bring herself
to wipe them away.

In one post from a few months before, James
had obviously not even taken the time to edit
himself, or to spell check; he had merely
poured his feelings out on to the page then hit
send, forever capturing his raw emotions.

Saturday, 4:12pm

I went to a memorial today at the Coral Lane Centre for my neighbours husband. Carl passed away two years ago and Dorothy had organised a trip to his favourite pub for his closets friends.

Dorothy and Carl had been togherther for 58 years. Dinah and I'd had just on five.

Dorothy and I have been spending time chatting over the back shrub a couple of times a week since Dinah passed away. We talk of about current affairs, we talk of Kane and how he is coping, nothing deep or specific, skirting around the issue... But it has been helpful all the same.

Even so, I wasn't sure if I would go to Carl's memorial, but in the end Dorothy called on me for help. 'James, dear,' she said. 'If you could give me a lift there my sister could bring me home.' How could I refuse? Even when I knew she wanted me there more for my sake than hers.

In the end I found that I was not nearly as stressed as I expected t be. I was nhumb. I felt nothing. But why? Why, when I know what Dorothy is going through cuold I not feel more remorse for her? Is it beacuse the well is dry?

Will I never feel anything any deeper than this hum of ever diminishing fuzzy memory ever again?

Siena put the rose back on the bedside table as she reached for a tissue.

Dorothy. She remembered Dorothy. A nice old lady even back when she had been a pre-teen. She'd always had a stash of passionfruit yogurt in the fridge in case Siena came a-calling. Oh, hell, Dorothy and Carl had been the ones to take her in when Rick had had to tend to the details the day her father died.

Feeling emotionally ragged, Siena decided enough was enough. She had a big day ahead of her and the last thing she needed was to wake with puffy red eyes.

She clicked back to the home page to find

James had left a post just that evening and she thought, *Okay, just one more.*

But the minute her gaze landed upon the first words she wished, and not for the first time in her life, that she wasn't so damned curious.

Thursday, 8:07pm

Today I met a girl.

Those words, and the unequivocal connotation that goes with them, haven't even entered my subconscious for nigh on six years.

Sure I have met women in that time— dozens, hundreds, even—colleagues, customers, strangers on the street, women working at banks, in shops. Kane's teachers and his new GP are all women.

But today, for the first time since I met Dinah, since I dated Dinah, since I loved her, and since she was taken from me, I met a girl.

Siena blinked. Once. Twice. A third time. But the words remained.

James Dillon had met a girl.

And, though no names were mentioned, no details given away, she knew it as well as she knew her own name.

That girl was her.

CHAPTER FIVE

THE next morning Siena sat in the lounge of her brother's body shop flicking unseeingly through grease-stained three-year-old car magazines.

After a restless night—dreaming repeatedly of a certain handsome carpenter sweating and straining as he bent over a workbench wearing naught but man-sized Osh Kosh denim overalls as he carved the words 'TODAY I MET A GIRL' into a baby changing table—she had woken to find a note from Rick saying he had found her dry cleaning ticket, taken it and would pick her outfit up for her on his way to an on-site job that morning.

After much hand-wringing at the fact that her interfering brother had wiped out the plans she had made to keep herself busy before Rufus was due to pick her up around one o'clock, she had wasted some time dolling herself up for her afternoon interview—hair blow-dried from a pert side parting and flicked at the ends, and make-up of the smoky eye, pink-cheeked and natural lip variety—and dressed in her jeans of the day before, beige and green layered tank tops and her red high heels, ready to change into her suit the minute it arrived back into her waiting arms, and caught a cab to the auto-mechanic to wait.

And wait. And wait.

'Siena?'

She turned, expecting to find another of Rick's kindly grease monkeys offering her another cup of undrinkable coffee while she waited, only to find the handsome carpenter himself standing by the couch.

She leapt to her feet. 'James!'

At her enthusiastic reaction, James's mouth kicked into a brief smile. Still only a half-smile but she swore she caught a glimpse of neat white teeth. Her heart rate doubled in an instant.

Gone were the dusty black T-shirt and worn jeans of the day before, and in their place he wore a white T-shirt, a lightweight grey linen jacket and dark grey trousers, all of which brought out faint streaks of blue in his silvery eyes. With one hand in his trouser pocket and his cheeks freshly shaved, the guy looked as if he had walked straight off the Spanish Steps.

'What…what are *you* doing here?' she asked, her voice rising.

'Matt told me where your brother worked,' James said, running a quick nervous hand over his short hair. 'I came on the off-chance you might be here. Or, if not, that they might tell me where you were. But you *are* here. So…here you are.'

'Here I am,' she agreed. Her heart leapt in her throat and she mentally slapped it down because, though he had no idea that she knew why he was there, she knew. And the reason terrified her to the soles of her Jimmy Choos.

'*Piccolo*,' her brother's voice boomed out from the office behind reception. 'Are you here? I'm heading out to pick up your suit now. I'll be another half hour at least. Do you want some cheese on crackers to get you by before lunch?'

Siena felt disaster looming. If Rick caught her with a *guy* there would be no living it down. But she was her own worst enemy on that count as her pause brought the bear from his cave, wiping his grease-stained hands on an old rag that looked dirtier than he was. 'Siena?'

When he saw her standing with James, the two of them looking equally guilty and nervous and unsure, he slowed. 'Well, what have we here?'

Siena grimaced at Rick before damping down her nerves, turning on a polite smile and introducing the two men. 'James, this is my big brother, Rick Capuletti, the owner of this fine establishment. Rick this is James Dillon—'

'The furniture guy,' Rick finished, flapping his rag at James.

'That's me.'

'Right. Right. With the big fancy show-room in town. My wife begged me until I bought your signature lamp tables. She had seen them in some celebrity magazine. Cost me a bloody packet.'

Siena looked back at James in redoubled surprise. The beautiful Queen Anne, art deco fusion lamp tables in Tina's lounge room were his design? The changing table in his workshop had been gorgeous. Delightful. But those lamp tables were beautiful. More than beautiful. They were works of art.

He smiled at Rick but the light barely reached his eyes. Hmm. Could it be that the glimmer and blue flecks and half-smiles weren't for everybody? She couldn't even begin to hide her mischievous delight.

'Pleased to meet you, Dillon,' Rick said, holding out a hand then retracting it when he saw how dirty it still was.

James saluted him. 'Consider it shook.'

Rick grinned, taking in Siena in its beaming light. 'How do you two kids know each other?'

Siena could barely contain her groan. *Here we go*, she thought, knowing he was about to start acting like a doting over-protective father. He couldn't help himself. All his life. Even when her poor dad had been alive.

She sucked in a deep breath, knowing the

next few would not come so easily as she began to suffocate under his rigid attention. 'The boy who I swerved to miss when I crashed the green monster was James's son,' she blurted.

'It turns out I bought your old family home,' James added, and Siena cursed under her breath for not cutting him off before she saw that titbit coming.

It would hardly take a rocket scientist to figure out that she had been cruising by the place on purpose. And after she had told him in no uncertain terms seven years before that she would never step foot in the place again as long as she lived.

She was fast learning that *never* was a much longer time than she had anticipated.

'Are you sure?' Rick asked, prolonging the agony. 'From what I remember, it went to a lady. Campbell? Diana Campbell?'

'Dinah,' James said, admirably keeping his voice even, but Siena could sense his whole body tightening.

She couldn't bear to look at either of them.

She could all but hear the echo of the train wreck on the horizon.

'Right. So you have a son, eh?' Rick asked.

'I do. Kane. He's eight.'

'I have two boys. Twins. And a new baby girl. A joy, aren't they?'

'They can be,' James said, his voice sliding back into its normal gentle rumble.

'So you're married, then?' Rick asked.

'Ah, no. I'm not. Not any more.'

'Divorced?'

'Rick!' Siena cried. It seemed that staring at her toes wasn't making it all go away.

Rick held up his hands in surrender. 'Okay. Fine. I am sorry,' he cried, his loud voice booming across the reception area.

'Rubbish. You're a meddlesome pain in the neck.'

'And you're not?'

'*Riccione!* Enough. He is so dramatic,' she said by way of apology, while still glaring at her brother, who glared right back. 'It's an Italian thing.'

And a big brother thing. And a Rick thing.

And a thing that sets my teeth on edge and makes my skin crawl so bad I just want to scratch and scratch until it goes away. Or I go away…

If James didn't realise that she was one half of a fruitless, ruinous, dysfunctional family and run for the hills rather than stand there looking so darned handsome, she would be very much surprised.

'Was there something you wanted from me?' she asked, turning to James, willing him to just leave and get it over with.

But the light that had been so absent in James's cool grey eyes since Rick had arrived on the scene had suddenly flared to life while she hadn't been paying attention. Siena bit her lip, wishing she had phrased her question differently.

'Well, yes, actually. I was heading out for a coffee and I thought perhaps you might join me as thanks for cleaning up Kane's wound yesterday.'

'A wound? My spoilt little sister working in a service industry seemed out of character enough, but now a real flesh and blood wound?' Rick said. 'Well, I never.'

Siena turned her back on her brother and shoved a hand through James's looped arm. 'Thanks, James. That would be nice. The coffee they serve in this place is criminal. Please tell me someone in this town knows how to make a real cappuccino.'

Without a backward glance, Siena turned James Dillon on his heel and, trying her best to ignore the heavenly scent of his woodsy aftershave, she marched him out the front door.

'I would watch yourself, mate,' Rick called out. 'She is as much of a hazard off the road as she is on it.'

It was all Siena could do not to grab one of the tyres piled up at the front door and fling it at him.

When she waved her hand back at her brother James thought he caught sight of a rude hand signal but he couldn't be sure. But even the concept was enough to create a flicker of laughter deep in his chest. A flicker was good. A flicker was promising. A flicker was more than he had felt in such a long time.

Which was why, even after making the decision not to come looking for her again, the minute the words had poured into his blog he had back-pedalled.

Those blog pages were his truth. The things he couldn't admit to anyone, not even himself. From the start he had always felt that if he lied on the page it would be defying the very point of the thing. And if his blog said to give it a chance, then he was willing to give it a chance.

As they turned out on to the main street, James could not help but notice the warm energy vibrating through his arm from where her soft hand clenched his elbow. He hadn't been imagining it the day before. Something chemical, or electrical, or biological happened to him when they came into close proximity. And who was he, a simple cabinet-maker, to argue with science?

But, now that he had confirmed it, he wasn't exactly sure what he was going to do next. He hadn't really thought past the asking.

He'd sent Kane off to school despite another 'headache'. He'd come to her, he'd asked her out and she'd said yes. Heck, those quacks would have fallen over themselves to see the progress he and Kane'd made in one single day!

He risked a glance at Siena. She had done something to her hair and the curls were smoothed away into a sassy bob. She wore make-up that made her eyes seem dark and deep, but no matter how she might be trying to hide beneath the flight attendant construct he knew that in a crowded room she would still stand out to him like a red umbrella in a sea of black.

Despite the warm feelings buoying him just being with her again, it didn't blind him to the fact that she wasn't a happy camper. Her brow was furrowed and her full lips stretched tight. She didn't look as if she was prepared for a nice coffee date. She looked like a kid playing spin the bottle who had ended up paired with her cousin. He reluctantly let her arm slide through his.

'Hey, Speedy Gonzales, where are we going?'

She slowed and only just seemed to remember he was there. 'Oh. Sorry. Is there somewhere along here we can grab a bite? I haven't eaten breakfast yet, and I kept refusing Rick's goons' offers of cheese and crackers and now I could eat a horse. And if I don't have a proper coffee in the next five minutes I won't be worth knowing.'

He had somewhere in mind but it would take longer than five minutes to get there. He weighed up the fiery temper of hers that he had just witnessed firsthand with the thought of having her in his company for longer than it would take her to throw down an espresso. Her company won out.

'Would you trade a mediocre takeaway coffee and a muffin now for a great cappuccino and the world's best bacon and eggs a tiny bit later? I promise it'll be worth it.'

Her focus shifted until he was caught in the intense light of her gaze. 'You're a man of mystery today, aren't you, Mr Dillon?'

'That I am. So what do you say?'

After a few moments of unintentionally enticing lip nibbling, she nodded.

'Great. Follow me.'

Fifteen minutes later, with their appetites subdued, they were queuing to board the famous Skyrail—a seven and a half kilometre cableway of over one hundred small, round, glassed-in capsules that could take six at a time up to the mountaintop town of Kuranda. And Siena was so hyperactive he wasn't sure he ought to come through with another coffee at the other end.

'I can't believe I'd forgotten all about this thing,' she said, jumping from one foot to the other on her high red heels, as they came closer to the front of the queue. 'It opened only a couple of years before I left. I would beg and beg and beg Rick to bring me up here, but he never did as he's afraid of heights, which is half the reason I begged and begged.'

She shot him a cheeky grin. 'You met him. He deserved it, right?'

'I'll say.'

A local in a khaki uniform helped the two of them into a small swinging capsule suspended from a fist-thick overhead wire, locked the glass door and told them to remember to 'smile at the frog' once they reached the other end.

'Smile at the what?' Siena asked and then her mouth dropped open as the concrete base slid away from under them and, just like that, they were hanging suspended over the rainforest. 'Holy heck!'

As she gripped on to her seat, her eyes huge in her face as she peered out the three hundred and sixty degree windows at the view unfolding as their capsule swung up the mountain, James leant back against the hot glass, crossed his arms and simply watched her.

She turned to him, her eyes questioning, and he couldn't help but smile back. 'We put on quite a show up here for the tourists,' he said.

'You can say that again. Wow, this is amazing! How long does it take to Kuranda?'

'Non-stop? About thirty-five minutes,' he said, which was a little longer than the 'tiny bit later' he had promised her.

He waited for her to explode at being kidnapped, which was pretty much what he had resorted to, unsure as he was that she was as far along in this attraction thing as he was, but she just nodded and continued to shift and shuffle to get the best view.

Their capsule swung back and forth with her movements. If she had been half as energetic as a teenager, he was sure big burly Rick Capuletti would have been green about the gills by that stage.

They bumped and trundled their way up the mountain in silence, masses of ferns and vines, hot red flame trees, towering conifers and thick dark rainforest vegetation sliding away secretively beneath them. When the grand Barron River peeked through the foliage, twinkling silver in the late morning sun, James spoke up.

'Get your land-legs back on. We're almost there.'

Siena looked back at him with a relaxed smile. Her cheeks were pink from her time in the sun and, for the first time since he had met her, she seemed loose-limbed and relaxed.

'If you tell me they've torn down the markets and those odd hippy shops to make way for a strip mall and condos I will take back everything I've ever believed about the snail pace progress of this place,' she said.

The tickle of laughter that had threatened earlier bubbled to the surface as he actually chuckled. 'Don't get too excited. You're still more likely to be able to pick up some weird herbal concoction at the markets than you are to find a Starbucks or McDonald's.'

'Great,' she said, beaming so suddenly that James's next breath lodged in his throat. 'I know just what to get Rick for Christmas!'

When their capsule reached the other end, a guide reminded them to 'smile at the frog', which turned out to be a frog-shaped camera. They did as they were told. Siena leaned in towards him, her shoulder brushing his as she smiled amiably until the flash went off.

Caught up in the heady feeling of companionship, James took a hold of Siena's dangling hand and wrapped it back into the crook of his arm and led her into town. She didn't argue or pull away, and when he glanced at her again he found the furrowed brow was clear. His cheek twitched into a self-satisfied smile.

She could stay that relaxed if she just allowed herself to live on tropics time, he thought.

James ducked into one shop alone and came out with a big floppy sun-hat to ward off the hot North Queensland sun.

'You can't,' she insisted when he gave it to her.

'I must,' he said. 'It cost five bucks, and remember I overcharge. Besides your nose is pink.'

Though it was a size too big, she gave in and slapped it atop her neat bob and he was sure she walked closer as they continued to window-shop.

Nestled in amongst the brightly coloured shop fronts selling tie-dyed clothes, local artwork and bric-a-brac sat Sloppy Joe's—a rundown café that looked as though the town had been built around it.

When they wandered into the empty room, the couple sitting smoking something sweet at the front table peeled themselves from their chairs. One pulled out a notepad and the other ambled into the kitchen.

'Busy day?' James asked the waitress, tongue firmly in cheek.

'Too busy for my liking,' the waitress agreed, then grinned at him through her chewing gum and pointed to a booth in the corner.

'Do you think the people in this place know what a cappuccino is?' Siena whispered, pulling off her hat and ruffling a hand up the back of her hair, which was beginning to curl despite the effort that had obviously gone into keeping it smooth.

'We'll soon find out.'

'Do you come here often?' Siena asked, her inquisitive eyes darting about the room, taking in the bright paintings for sale on the dark walls, the unswept concrete floor and slow-moving ceiling fans pushing the humid heat around the room.

'Not for ages. My grandad was a cabinet-maker before me and he ran a stall at the markets up here. He swore by their all-day breakfast. But that was a while back.'

'Did he teach you everything you know?' she asked, sliding into the vinyl booth, which squeaked as she sat.

'Not everything,' he said. Again he heard a note of flirtation which was unintended. Okay, so maybe this time it was.

Maybe he wanted to know if she realised that he had taken a huge leap in inviting her out for *coffee*. The night before he'd confessed to her about Dinah, and he was all but sure she wasn't oblivious to the effect she had on him.

Siena blinked back at him. His whole body warmed under her direct gaze before she grabbed the jar of sugar and twirled the cut glass distractedly around and around between her palms.

'What can I getcha?' the waitress—who looked as though she had probably worked there back in the day—asked when she arrived at their table.

'Two cappuccinos and two breakfast specials?' James asked.

'Perfect,' Siena said shortly, all her earlier ease dissipated. Something had definitely spooked her. She wasn't the same free and easy girl from the day before. Now she looked as nervous as he felt.

The waitress gave them a smile and a wink, before tucking her notebook in the waist of her skirt and her pencil back behind her ear and sauntering off to the kitchen.

And then they were alone. Alone. On a date. Of sorts. James and a girl. A woman. A lovely woman. A woman who was obviously for some reason second-guessing being there with him.

As Siena looked about the room, her skittish glance landing on everything but him, he wondered what the hell he had been thinking when he'd woken up that morning.

But, since he had always been pathologically intent on making the best of things, he asked, 'What did you call your brother earlier? Rigatoni?'

As intended, the sideways barb at her brother brought about a flash of a smile. She shoved the sugar back against the wall and started flicking through the pile of paper napkins.

'My brother and cousin and I were all named after towns in Tuscany,' she said, 'where our parents were all born. Rick is Riccione. My cousin Ash is actually Asciano, and I am, well, Siena.'

He had to stop himself from reaching out and laying a hand over hers to stop her fidgeting, but her nerves were all of a sudden running so hot he had the feeling she might spontaneously combust if he tried.

'It's a beautiful name,' he said, trying to get a reaction from her that wasn't born of nervous tension. She was giving off so much energy that even his usually solid on the ground feet tapped beneath the table. 'It suits you.'

Her mouth curled in what was meant to be a smile, but to him it seemed more of a sort of grimace, and he felt himself deflating.

He'd made a huge mistake.

He'd been reading into things she had said and done that simply mustn't have been there. Maybe she was just a really good listener and it had been such a long time since he'd talked to anyone about his life, bar his blog. Just because he felt things, new things, deep down things, when he was with her, didn't mean she felt the same way.

He'd gone way out of his comfort zone, relying on gut instinct rather than on what he had been told by experts would be best for him and Kane, and it seemed his instincts weren't what they used to be.

He was fast thinking that science left a lot to be desired when Siena suddenly looked his way. Like a heat-seeking missile that had found its target, their gazes clashed, jolted, and told James a lot more about the situation than either of them were likely to admit aloud after such a short acquaintance.

He felt as though fireworks were going off in his stomach. And he knew then that he hadn't in fact been thinking a whole lot when he'd woken up that morning. Not with his head, anyway.

Siena couldn't look away. It was the train wreck thing again. James's eyes were still masked by a layer of melancholy, but there was an almost grim determination behind them today. As if he had seen a way through the sadness and had latched on for all his might.

And, though she was deadly afraid that he mistakenly thought that *she* might be the way through, *nobody* had ever looked at her that way before.

She was the delinquent little sister, the aggressively ambitious worker or the exotic Aussie stranger in town for one night only. Reflected in his soulful eyes she saw herself as so much more.

No. Nope. Na-uh. Bad news.

She *never* should have used him as an escape route from Rick, after he had confided in her about Dinah and especially after reading what he had written in his blog the night before.

But she had been so caught up in his scent and the feel of her hand hooked into his strong arm and the promise of a trip on the Skyrail that she had blissfully forgotten that James was not a *casual friendship* guy.

He was a guy with roots and responsibility and a family, and she was a walking disaster.

A destroyer of families. A deserter. Too much hard work. And someone who could not be trusted to take on the responsibility of someone else's life.

She had to turn him away, gently but in such a way that he knew it was for the best. So she said the one thing she knew would do it.

'Tell me more about Dinah.'

She waited for him to hang his head in sadness, but his deep grey eyes remained clear and locked on to hers.

Okay, so maybe if she shut up he would gush and blather on about Dinah for an hour and a day like newly divorced people she knew tended to, then after a while he would realise he had been blathering and he would be embarrassed by said blathering and he would slink away after their coffee and never seek her out again.

'What in particular would you like to know about her?' he asked, taking a measured sip of still water, but with his eyes never leaving hers.

Okay, so not so much blathering. Instead of blathering his sensuous mouth kicked up at one corner. The wretch *knew* she was *really* asking about Dinah because she was actually interested in *him*.

'I…I saw her photo on your piano when I was snooping about the house. I'm a snoop. There. I admit it. It's a terrible habit of mine. Incurable. Immoral. But that's just me. Anyway, there was a photo of Dinah. She seemed much like Kane,' she said, and was quite pleased with her save, especially since she was able to make herself seem completely irresponsible into the bargain. 'What was she like?'

'Dinah was…' He looked at the ceiling for a few moments as he searched for the word. 'Incandescent.'

Siena felt her stomach drop to her knees.

Incandescent? Did the guy seriously say *incandescent*? Well, if he had been punishing her for masking her attraction to him by using the dead wife card, he sure didn't pull his punch.

Nobody had ever called *her* incandescent before. Cute, maybe. Single-minded, sure. A pain in the ass, often. But incandescent? What kind of man even *thought* to search for a word so beautiful? A creator of exquisite, inventive, deliciously cedar oil scented works like the man who had invited her out for coffee and then taken her on a ride through the sky, that was who.

'Kane does look like her,' he continued, finding something outside the window suddenly fascinating.

She wanted to grab him by the chin until he looked back at her again, all sparkling and almost smiling.

'I have always thought Kane's temperament was much more like mine,' he continued. 'Maybe that's the bane of the adoptive dad, searching for personality traits that aren't really there.'

'He seems a really…nice kid,' Siena said, choosing her words more carefully as she dragged herself up out of a pit of sudden unseemly jealousy. 'I'm sure that's a great deal thanks to you.'

Nice? Yep, nice was a good safe word. But, even as she lauded herself for her vocabulary brilliance, James looked back at her, his mouth kicking up at one corner, and he gave her a short nod, accepting her words as though they were a high compliment, which of course they really were.

Argh!

Their food arrived and Siena could have hugged the over-tanned wrinkly waitress who had obviously seen too much Far North Queensland sun in her lifetime.

She drank the cappuccino in one hit to reorganise her nerves and regretted it instantly. Firstly, James had been right, it was delicious, on par with those she'd had in Rome. And, secondly, it scalded her mouth so that the juicy-looking bacon and eggs on her plate would now no doubt taste like burnt taste buds.

Excellent.

James ate his meal without dropping a crumb. She tried to do the same and failed. She always ate too fast, had too much sauce or too much bread left at the end and at least one dollop of tomato seeds that missed her plate altogether. But James seemed to understand how to do everything in the perfect time with perfect portions.

He even had a sip of no doubt lukewarm cappuccino left to spare at the end.

'So what about your family?' he asked, after dabbing at the corners of his crumb-free mouth. 'Do your parents still live around here?'

Siena quickly ran her tongue around her teeth, checking for sesame seeds. 'Um, oh, no. I was a late…surprise.'

She was going to leave it there, but the fact that he had been brave enough to tell her about Dinah the night before made her feel it would be unfair not to be as honest. 'There were complications and my mum, well, she passed away having me.'

His eyes narrowed, brimming with such sudden flaring compassion that Siena leant back in her chair to escape it.

'It must have been difficult, growing up without your mum.'

Siena waved a hand over her face. 'I survived. I had an older brother with the requisite eyes in the back of his head. Besides, you can hardly miss what you never had.'

Whereas Kane would, she suddenly realised. The poor thing knew exactly what he was missing not having his sunshiny, *incandescent* mother on the scene any more. Siena's heart reached out to the sweet kid.

Stop it! Her heart did *not* reach. Not to handsome single dads with half-smiles and manly hands and cavernous grey eyes, and certainly not to their kids, even if said kids did not drink cola and their sticky warm hands felt so trusting and small in her own that she actually missed them like a phantom limb when they were gone.

She rubbed her hands together to erase that sense memory and went back to picking at a piece of stray bacon with the end of her fork.

'And your father?' he asked.

'My dad died when I was fifteen,' she said, rolling her right shoulder to ease away the tension that always encroached during the rare times she talked of that part of her life.

'How?' James asked, not even pretending to blather inanities as others always had. If only she could be as accepting, but ten years and a heck of a lot of guilt, regret, recrimination and fast living later, the memory still felt as though it was eating her from the inside out.

'I was a handful as a kid, and that's putting it mildly. Dad had a big heart; I gave it cause to worry and one day it finally gave out,' she said simply.

'Rubbish,' James said, catching her so unawares she didn't even have time to get her back up. 'You had no control over how much your dad worried about you, Siena, or how he chose to deal with it. Not a lick. Handful or angel child, his heart was built to worry about you and to love you, not to collapse because you learned how to swear a year or two before your friends did.'

He had a smile in his eyes as he spoke, and for a second she almost believed him and the resulting weight off her shoulders made her feel as though she was levitating an inch off her chair. *He* was a parent. *He* had a troubled kid. *He* ought to know…

But Kane was only eight, she remembered, returning to the squeaky vinyl seat with a thud. Not even yet a teen. She wondered if she ought to give James details on how much worse she had been, and how much worse Kane could get. But somehow she couldn't convince herself to take the rare shine from those divine grey eyes.

'And big brother Rick became your guardian, I take it,' James said.

Her mouth twitched. 'He took to it like a croc to tropical waters. You may have noticed that telling me what to do is more of a vocation than a burden for Rick.'

'That's what big brothers are for.'

'Doesn't mean I have to like it.'

He leaned forward, his head moving to within a bare foot of hers. 'So if you are a determined nomad as your brother attests, what has brought you back home now?'

Home. Siena waited for the word to make her nauseous. But the way the word sounded in James's deep soothing voice, though there was a definite tingle in her stomach, for the first time since she'd hopped on the plane the day before she didn't feel like throwing up.

'I have an interview with Maximillian himself late this very afternoon.' She looked at her watch and something twisted inside her as she realised they would soon have to head back so she could get ready.

'Right. MaxAir's head office is in Port Douglas,' James said. 'I was commissioned to do a piece for him for that house of his up there a couple of years back. That's some pad,' he said, his voice doing that low, intimate thing he was so good at that seemed to wash over every inch of bare skin.

She leant back in her chair as far as she was able but she still felt his woodsy scent enveloping her.

'Not a changing table, I would hazard to guess.' It had never been any secret to anyone who had ever known him that Maximillian was gay.

'Ah, no. So this meeting with Max,' he said. 'Has he brought you up this way to try to convince you to stay? I have met several executives of his who were lured up here for job opportunities who have never left. That seems to be his routine.'

The cloud of warmth that had been slowly

but surely curling around Siena faded out of sight. *That* was exactly what she was afraid of. Her crew had even put big money bets on it. 'I don't actually know what Max wants with me.'

'What would be the ideal?'

'Rome,' she said, without even a hint of hesitation. 'It's the pinnacle. The top job. I want it so bad I can taste it.'

Well, she couldn't taste anything after her hot coffee but she could remember what it tasted like.

A sudden shadow passed over James's eyes and, knowing she had been the cause, Siena had to look away. She made a great play at looking at her watch. 'And, speaking of Max, I actually should head back soon.'

James motioned to the waitress for the bill.

When Siena reached for her Visa card, which always lived in the back pocket of her jeans, he stayed her with a waggling finger. Siena watched it as if it was a metronome before putting her credit card away.

'This is my treat,' he said.

'Wow, you're a man of a different era,' Siena said, trying to keep it light. 'The guys I usually date offer to pay half plus the tip at best.'

Date? Had she just admitted to James that she saw this as a date? Faced with a nice suit and a clean shave her sense had been left by the wayside.

'Nah,' he said, a smile tickling at the corners of his mouth as he forked over a couple of notes after glancing at the menu prices. 'You can pay next time.'

Next time? A wry smile? Oh, curses!

James slid out of the bench seat and held out a hand to help her out of hers. She took it, proud that she kept her breathing to a pretty reasonable canter as his warm fingers closed about hers. He tugged her slowly until her legs were free of the table, and then he didn't let go.

He twisted his fingers until they were held together by the lightest touch, so that he could navigate an easy way for the two of them through the wide, empty aisles between sporadic tables.

He looked over his shoulder at one stage, caught her eye and smiled again. Trapped by the genuine pleasure in his gaze, Siena couldn't help but smile back, her cheeks growing pink and warm like a school girl with her first crush.

Once they hit sunshine he put her big hat back on her head and tucked her hand through his elbow once more, drawing her against his warm body, and this time he left his hand curled over hers. His strong, callused, sublimely warm hand.

I am leaving tomorrow! she screamed inside her head when he turned back to face the front. That was all she had to say. *Saturday afternoon I will be on a flight to Melbourne and I have no immediate plans to return soon, if ever.* But somehow she couldn't get the words to form on her tongue.

Because she'd had a nice time. A really, genuine, honest-to-goodness nice time. Talking, connecting, debating, retreating, learning interesting snippets about another person, a person who kept her on her toes and made her feel all warm and yummy and inter-esting and good, and encroaching on issues one would never usually get to on such a short acquaintance.

But maybe it was the fact that she would be leaving the next day that made it all happen so fast. They didn't have time to skirt any issues.

And for all her friends the world over, the casual gentlemen with whom she wined and dined and talked superficial gossip, from elegant Gage to cheeky Raoul, the sky girls who could go days without sleep so they could get the most out of a New York layover, she felt as though if she added every fabulous outing together it would never add up to as much warm satisfaction as she had taken out of this irregular little lunch.

In the future, if she was in need of a happy place to go to in order to settle her nerves when frustration kicked in, this would be it—palm trees, colourful shops, blue skies and a warm arm to hang on to.

By the time they reached the Kuranda Skyrail station, she had almost convinced herself that maybe James could be her Cairns *friend*. If she came back here every now and again, maybe they could make it a habit of going out for coffee in weird and wonderful local haunts. It would be fun! More than fun; it would be lovely.

But then snippets of his blog came swimming back to her like pieces of her own conscience.

There are days when the thought of going outside the front door leaves me in a cold sweat.

A guy who had got himself all dressed up to take her out for a cup of coffee wasn't looking for *fun*, even if he had convinced himself otherwise. He wasn't even anywhere close to looking for lovely. Whatever he was looking for, *she* didn't have the capacity to give it to him.

After a quiet, reflective trip back down the mountain to Cairns they again reached the pile of tyres at the front of Rick's Body Shop.

Siena pulled James to a halt. There was no

way she wanted him taking her inside under the beady eyes of her brother.

'Okay, so this is me.'

James nodded, his eyes unreadable as he looked over every inch of her face. 'Good luck with your interview,' he said. 'I hope the news is good.'

But she knew from the glimmer in his eyes that his idea of *good* was pretty much the opposite of hers.

'Thanks,' she said. Her natural restlessness tickled at her toes. The fact that this was goodbye made her even more fidgety than usual as she bounced on the balls of her feet.

A slight smile warmed James's serious face, then, without warning, he leant into her. Pure instinct took over as Siena stopped all semblance of bouncing and her eyes closed as she sank into the sensation of his warm smooth cheek against hers. His hand curled around her waist for balance. Hers fluttered to rest against his solid chest.

'Thanks for coffee, Siena. I'll see you again soon,' he murmured, his deep voice humming against her ear, causing skitters of sensation down her whole right side.

His lips pressed against her cheek, burning an imprint she feared no amount of scrubbing would make disappear, and then he pulled back.

After one last keen look, as though he was committing her face to memory, he turned and walked away, leaving Siena feeling as if she wasn't quite sure if she could remember how to put one foot in front of the other to get where she needed to go.

CHAPTER SIX

'So how was your big date?' Matt asked, through the flywire screen he was busy cleaning, as James came through the front door of his Apple Tree Drive home.

James all but jumped out of his skin. 'Don't do that, mate! Seriously!'

He threw his keys on to the hall table and continued through to the kitchen, where he buried his head in the fridge though he wasn't quite sure what he hoped to find in there other than a place to hide from Matt.

But, alas, that wasn't to be. Matt's head appeared over the top of the fridge. 'Don't leave me hanging.'

'It wasn't a date, Matt,' James said, reaching for an apple he didn't really want. 'I just met her for coffee to thank her for patching Kane up yesterday.'

'You could have fooled me, Jimbo. What with the jacket and all, if I didn't know you were meeting with her, I would have thought you were off to a day with the investors.'

James looked down at his outfit. 'You're imagining things.'

Matt reached out suddenly. James ducked away but he was too late to stop Matt from swiping a finger along his cheek. Matt smelled his finger. 'Aftershave. The good stuff. Did I also imagine you had left the ironing board open?'

James stifled an oath and slowly bit into the apple as a big goofy smile grew on Matt's lined face.

'It's okay, dude. It was an amateur's mistake. Now spill. How did it go?'

James slumped into a chair by the round kitchen table. It had been a day filled with many firsts—his first *date* in several years, the first time he had found a woman whose hand fitted into his as though it was made to be there, and the first time he had ever told *anyone* how much he hoped Kane was like him. *Anyone…*

'It was strange,' James admitted, trying the words on his tongue rather than on his fingertips, and finding they didn't taste as sharp and hurtful as he had expected they might. 'Terrifying, mystifying and enjoyable by turns.'

'Fantastic!'

'Fantastic?' He shuffled higher on the chair. 'Matt, I have no idea what I was even thinking. Kane still stays up talking through his day to Dinah before he goes to sleep, and every morning is still spent in hope he'll go to school without some sort of hypochondriac complaint. I'm not sure he's anywhere near ready for anything of this sort.'

'In all those lame excuses you didn't say one word about how *you* feel about this girl.'

James let that comment lie.

'Am I trying too hard? Trying to get back to the dating scene like it's part of some twelve step programme to becoming a proper human being again? When really, maybe, I don't ever *have* to go through it all again.'

All that feminine mystique. All those girls' nights out wondering if this time she might not come home at all. And all that pain in wondering that if he had done more to try to stop her, to tame her, to need her the way she needed him, everything might have turned out differently.

'Okay. That's a fair point,' Matt said, straddling the chair next to James. 'But answer me this: why now?'

'What do you mean?'

'Have you been thinking about your twelve step theory for some time? Or is this the first time it has occurred to you?'

James wasn't entirely sure. He had touched on it in his blog, but it had always been a rhetorical argument. A question sent out into the void with no hope of a response.

'I hadn't really considered it in detail until now,' he admitted.

'You mean you hadn't considered it in detail until you met *her*?'

James let the words tumble about in his mind

until he was pretty sure that was exactly the right answer. He dropped his face into his palms.

'Fine. Then tell me why when she asked me about Dinah I said that she was incandescent.'

Matt laughed so hard his whole body shook. 'You told her Dinah was *what*?

'Incandescent. It means—'

'I know what it means. I also know that to be putting stuff like that out there on a first date you are either terrified of how much you like this girl or the complete opposite. And only you can know which.'

Matt patted him on the shoulder, then stood and left him to his thoughts.

His thoughts? His thoughts weren't the problem. It was his conscience that was having trouble keeping up.

'So how was your big date?' Rick asked Siena when she came out of the body shop staff bathroom all dolled up in her now cola-free Dolce suit, looking and feeling much more like herself than she had in the last twenty-four hours.

'It wasn't a date,' she said, as she ran a finger around the edge of her lips to make sure her lip gloss was picture perfect.

She swung her Kelly bag into the cracked vinyl lounge chair in Rick's office before following in its wake, letting her legs flop straight out in front of her and slinging an arm over her tired eyes.

She heard Rick sit down in his bouncy office chair on the other side of his big messy desk.

'If that nice James Dillon had anything to do with it, that was a date,' he said. 'Though I don't know what you two are playing at, Siena. He has a kid and he never did answer me properly about his wife.'

She shifted her arm and glared up at him. 'He's a *single* dad, Rick. His wife died over a year ago, but I hardly wanted to bring that up while introducing you to the guy. God, Rick. What sort of person do you think I am?'

'I see you so infrequently, Siena,' he said, his face hard, 'I'm sure I wouldn't know.'

'Well, know that I would *never* date a married man, or actively *not date* one, as the case may be. And, to put your troubled mind at rest, I have no intention of throwing my terrible self at *nice* James Dillon either. I'm leaving tomorrow. There would be no point.'

'So how about your fellow in New York? Why didn't the fact you were leaving the next day stop you from hanging out with him?'

She glared at him from beneath her arm to find him spinning a grimy old soccer ball on the end of his finger. 'James asked me out because he is a kind man and I agreed because I have seen enough of your ugly mug for one visit!'

Rick rocked back in his chair and watched her. 'Here we go again.'

'What's that supposed to mean?'

'You bounce about like a jumping bean while here, and bounce away before anything gets too settled. But this Dillon guy sees past the jumping bean, and that's a rare quality. Probably more than you deserve.'

And *there* he was—the Rick she had run from the minute she'd had the chance. She was shocked it had taken him all of twenty-four hours to tell her she was worthless.

Siena's blood quickly reached boiling point. Rick had cast off enough such throwaway comments at her as a kid that she had begun to believe them.

But she had shown him that she was better than that. She had shown the world she was better than that. She had flown into town for a personal meeting with Maximillian, for goodness' sake! If that didn't show Rick that she was deserving, then she had no idea what would.

Siena tried to sit up to defend herself but Rick threw the football at her and she slumped back into the couch, trapped and winded.

'He's a keeper, Siena,' Rick continued. 'He's financially successful and, according to the girls who were watching you guys leave, he is—and I quote—a "hottie". Don't do a typical you and blow him off like you've blown off everyone else who has tried to get close to you.'

She managed to pull herself upright and keep

her skirt from hiking under her armpits at the same time. 'I don't blow people off,' she said.

'That's exactly what you do, Siena. You couldn't give Dad the time of day from the second you became a teenager.'

I was a teenager! she wanted to scream. All teenage girls go through that cringe against their father. Especially ones who had always been daddy's little girl. That *didn't* mean that it was her fault that his heart had given way…

'Heck, you tried to blow me off long ago,' Rick said, 'and you would have succeeded if I didn't give you free rein on the end of a long rubber band. But I always knew you could never fly so far away that you would never spring back.'

'Please! You have nothing on me.'

'Of course I do. I am your family. As is my wife, who adores you. As are the twins, and I can see how your face turns all soft whenever they call you 'Enna. And, as to little Rosie— she looks so like you did as a baby it brings tears to my eyes.'

'Hang on a minute—'

'Siena, do you really think you can pull anything over on me any more?'

She had tried, so many times, to break the pull and tug of authority and self-reliance that had framed her childhood, and in leaving she had always thought she'd won the tug-of-war for good. But now she was back she knew the war had never been over, it had just been an intermission.

A knock came at the door. It was one of Rick's employees. 'Um, yeah, hi. There's a guy here in a blue suit and a funny hat who says he's here for your sister.'

Siena stood and placed the football carefully on his desk to show Rick exactly how much more mature than him she was. 'That will be Rufus. My driver. Thanks.'

The guy blushed beneath the grease streaks on his cheeks and left.

She waited for Rick to make some smart comment—wondering why she hadn't used her driver the day before rather than crashing his car—but he instead let go of a long high whistle.

'Well, you'd better fly. As always.'

* * *

'Afternoon, Rufus,' she said as he opened the back door of the thankfully air-conditioned limo for her.

'Ms Capuletti. You really should have called me to drive you to your old neighbourhood yesterday,' Rufus said as she slid into the back seat. 'You could have been hurt.'

She thought she heard the words 'women drivers' muttered under his breath as he shut the door but she was too shocked to care.

'*You* heard about that?' she asked when he got behind the wheel. She shuffled forward to lean on the open partition between them.

'I know a guy who knows a guy,' he said, watching her in the rear-view mirror, his beady blue eyes actually almost smiling, but Siena was pretty sure she didn't want to know about the marginal kinds of guys Rufus knew.

She sat back with a groan. Really this place was just so small town it made her sick.

'Oh, just shut up and drive, Rufus,' she said.

He laughed before gunning the engine. 'Yes, Ms Capuletti.'

The drive up to the beaches of Far North Queensland was glorious. They passed the Skyrail with its tiny round pods taking tourists by the hundreds slowly up the almost vertical cliffs covered in lush green vegetation towering forbiddingly to her left. For that lovely trip alone she knew she would now never regret having come back to Cairns.

With a deep breath she tuned that out and looked deliberately to her right where perfect white sandy beaches blinked between black rocky outcrops and intermittent tracts of sugar cane farms and banana plantations slowly growing anew after the devastation of a tropical cyclone.

They passed Palm Cove, a haven of resorts, lavish gardens and beachside bliss. In an alternate past she would have not called Rick and would have stayed there instead, working on her tan, spending the day at a resort spa or taking a boat out to Green Island for a glorious day snorkelling.

She couldn't help sitting higher in her leather seat to get a glimpse of the ocean, laid out blue and green and magnificent all the way out to the far horizon. She had to admit that of all the beaches in all the world this area was as beautiful as any she had ever known, and she had known a few. And most people would think themselves blessed to be surrounded by palm trees and year-round sunshine.

A half hour later the car slowed as they reached Port Douglas.

They passed the pristine manicured lawns of the world class golf course, hooked a right towards the beach, then a left through a set of large guarded gates. At the end of a straight white gravel driveway sat the palatial Palazzo Maximillian. It was a grand, symmetrical, three-storeyed, white and gold monstrosity sur-rounded by ubiquitous Queensland palm trees.

Maximillian, bald and tanned from head to toe, met her at the car door in a smoking jacket and white satin trousers and carrying a martini. Siena wondered if he was in fact waiting for a camera crew rather than just little old her.

As he drew her into his home, she shot one last look to the front driveway to find Rufus and the safety of his limousine heading back out the distant guarded gates.

'Siena,' Max drawled, his broad American accent evident even in that one word. 'Glad you could come.'

'No worries, Max,' she said, doing her best to act cooler than she felt.

'And do call me Max,' he said.

Siena groaned under her breath, counted to ten in her head in an attempt to control her breathing and yelled at herself mentally to *just relax*!

He pointed the way through his massive marble-floored foyer to the back of his house where a huge crystal blue pool lay shimmering in the golden afternoon sun.

She had a good look at the man behind the name. He was handsome. Tall, imposing, dripping in money. But, for all that, he had nothing on the understated magnetism of James Dillon.

Focus!

So you like James, she said to herself. *So you have a little crush on the guy. Okay, so it's more than a crush. The way he looks at you makes your poor little heart flutter. You've admitted it. Good for you; now shelve it.*

Max led the way to a couple of deep-set white cane chairs beneath a wide baby-blue umbrella. The view to one side was all golf course and, to the other, ocean as far as the eye could see.

'So, Siena,' he drawled when they sat, 'I would think that, considering the world class rumour mill working at MaxAir, you have some idea why I have asked you to meet me here today.'

Siena nodded, but she kept her mouth shut. Though rumours did tend to be true, she had no intention of putting her foot in her mouth any more that day than necessary.

Max's wide mouth broke into a blindingly white smile. 'Fabulous, so this will be a quick meeting. Siena, I have been more than pleased with the result of our recent teaser campaign featuring your face in billboards across Australia. It seems yours is a face that gives consumers confidence.'

Oh, God here it was—he was about to ask her to stay!

But what would she say if Max offered her the permanent job as face of MaxAir? Would she beg him for Rome? If he said no, would she quit?

She suddenly had no idea.

But she did know that something in her felt changed, and she did know that, no matter what Max offered her, she would not go back to the regular old routes that a few days before had been fine. A few days ago they had been ample. They had been great. They had been enough.

But now she wanted…more.

Siena's fingernails dug into her hot palms as she watched and waited. Her heart thundered in her chest.

'You may have heard that our Rome/Paris run,' Max continued, 'the leg that MaxAir began with ten years ago, the run of my heart, has been taking a beating from some of the other bigger carriers over the past year. As such I want you there. I want an injection of delightful Australian youth. I want you to turn Rome on its head.'

Siena waited for the other shoe to drop, the

shoe that was all about promotions and Cairns and staying put, when a waiter in a white suit appeared from nowhere with a fresh Martini for him and a pitcher of ice-cold lemon-flavoured water and a tumbler for her.

'I will be basing you out of Rome,' he said after the waiter disappeared as quietly as he had arrived, 'putting you up in your own apartment. I like my Rome girls to be fresh so you need not work more than three days out of seven and two months out of three. I look after my Rome girls, Siena, so if you thought you were flying high now, you have no idea what you are in for.'

Her thundering heart dropped to her stomach, creating a hollow ache deep behind her ribs.

Rome. After all her worrying and concern and soul-searching, Max was actually giving her Rome—her dream, the pinnacle, the position that would prove to all and sundry that she had really made it.

'Why me?' she asked, suddenly unable to stop herself from looking as stunned as she felt.

Max smiled at her ingenuous question, though it never quite reached his eyes.

'In all of our market research, you were consistently the number one most recognised face of all the boys and girls we have used over the spring. Your performance reviews have been consistently excellent. You have changed routes, crews, positions over and again without blinking an eye, without taking family concerns or boyfriends, or any of that jazz, into consideration as many of my girls have. You probably have no idea that you've only had—' he looked down at a piece of paper that Siena hadn't even noticed was there '—two sick days in seven years.'

It hit her as if he had just thrown the pitcher of ice-cold water in her face—the reason she'd never said no to a challenge was because, whereas her colleagues had been living well-rounded lives, she'd never *had* family concerns, or boyfriends, or any of that jazz to consider. Since the day she had run away from home she had kept on running and somehow she'd found herself employee of the millennium.

And suddenly she wasn't sure *why* she wanted to be that person after all.

When she didn't answer, Max's eyes narrowed and his smile broadened. He unfolded a piece of paper on MaxAir baby-blue stationery, grabbed a gold pen from a hidden pocket in his smoking jacket, made a few alterations to the page, then slid it over to her face up. 'This is my offer.'

Her head told her not to look, told her that it would be too good to be true and that she would drop to her knees and kiss his toes, while her heart told her to think on it.

But she was a sticky beak of the worst sort. Always would be. So she looked.

The money was double what she earned now. She would have free airfares with MaxAir anywhere any time for the extent of her contract. She would continue to have a driver—which Rick and Rufus would both be thrilled to hear!—and a moving allowance to take her to Rome within the week, which was why she hadn't been emailed a new schedule.

The deal was so good a mighty swear word slipped loudly from her mouth.

Max grinned. 'Do I take that as a yes?'

Siena's mind was tripping. Overloaded. The deal was something that most people would have accepted without a second thought. It was a deal that a week before *she* would have accepted without a second thought.

For all Max's kind words about loyalty, she was suddenly proving herself hard work. Trouble. Inconsistent. Just as Rick had accused her of being all these years.

She took the piece of paper, folded it twice and popped it into her handbag. 'How long do I have to think about it?'

Max's smile faded, but only slightly, before beaming back at her ever brighter. 'Twenty-four hours ought to do it.'

She nodded. A day. She had her last day in Cairns to think about it. 'I'll have an answer by this time tomorrow.'

Max stood and shook her hand.

Siena felt a presence behind her. Rufus was back. She realised that meant it was time to go.

She grabbed her handbag and followed Rufus, wondering how he survived in a three-piece suit on a day such as this. She was sweating and weak under the heat of her cream summer-weight tweed. Or maybe she was trembling because she had just been handed her dream on a platter and found she needed time to think about it.

'How did it go, Ms Capuletti?' Rufus asked when they reached the huge marble lobby.

'Perfect,' she moaned.

He shot her a sideways glance, his beady eyes burning into her, and again she wondered if he was only moonlighting in this job until the army needed him for some special operation.

'How do you feel about Rome?' he asked and she was no longer surprised that he knew everything before anyone else did.

'I love Rome. I adore Rome. The Trevi Fountain, the shopping, the cappuccinos, the prestige… It's what I've always wanted. And I told Max I have to think about it. Am I nuts? Should I run back in there now and tell him I was kidding and yes please and thank you and I'll pack the minute I get home?'

Rufus held open the limo door for her. 'No,'

he said. 'Make him wait. He doesn't get that nearly enough.'

He smiled, and it highlighted a long crazy scar on his right cheek, but Siena still smiled back. She had long since decided Rufus was a good person.

'Max's new training facilities are on the property,' he said. 'He thought you might like a tour while you're here.'

She nodded, thankful that she had a bit of time to collect herself. Rufus drove her to the training rooms which were located in a big blue and white office building just outside the security gates.

Inside they were glossy, retro-looking and state-of-the-art. And, despite herself, she was impressed. Seven years before, she had done her training in a rented office block on the outskirts of a dodgier suburb of Melbourne. She and Max had both come a long way since then.

'You are Siena Capuletti, aren't you?' someone asked from behind her.

Siena turned to find a group of bright-eyed, bushy-tailed trainees, all clones of Jessica of the bendy straw and juggling fascination. 'Yeah, I'm Siena.'

'When those new ads started running,' the blondest one said, 'we had bets going that you weren't really a sky girl for MaxAir. None of us had seen you on our runs. So are you really one of us?'

'Seven-year veteran at your service. I've done mixed overseas runs for the last three years, so maybe that's why we haven't met.'

'I would just die to get an overseas run,' Blondie said, her eyes misting over all dreamy.

And then Siena noticed the tiny diamond glittering on the young woman's left ring finger. She felt a momentary shot of empathy for the poor girl. That was never going to happen.

A flight attendant's life was transitory. Living out of a tiny suitcase. Working odd hours. No opportunity to settle down. All things which had attracted Siena in the first place. But for a young woman in love?

A MaxAir girl's version of love was getting pinched on the backside by a commuter. Or being offered gifts of lost property by baggage handlers. Or having a guy in every port...

'I know this seems silly,' Blondie said, 'but could I grab your autograph?'

'Sure.' Siena signed away. She didn't have the heart to tell the girl how hard it was going to be.

'Happy trails,' the girls called out in unison as Rufus beckoned her to the entrance.

'Same to you,' Siena said before walking off into the bright afternoon sunshine, feeling strangely sad, as if the trail beneath her feet was like a pure beach after high tide.

The only set of footprints on her beach to date were hers.

CHAPTER SEVEN

As Rufus took Siena through bright, cheerful downtown Cairns, she strove to remind herself why she hated this place so much.

They drove alongside the boardwalk, past market stalls, happy shiny people in bikini tops, short shorts and flip-flops, and the massive created lagoon perched amidst park-lands on the water's edge. Sleek tanned tourists lolled about on brightly coloured towels while young families splashed about in the shallows. Eye-catching restaurants and cafés and shops lined the beachside road.

The place had really changed in seven years. And so, she was beginning to realise, had she.

She wasn't the rebellious, confused, angry teenager she had once been. She had forged a great life for herself, a wonderful career, friends the world over, yet something was missing. Her wanderlust had taken her this far, but now her feet didn't feel itchy any more; they merely felt weary.

When they neared a familiar T-junction on the outskirts of Cairns, Siena called out, 'Rufus.'

'Change of plan, Ms Capuletti?'

The guy was a mind-reader! 'Actually, yes. I need you to do me a favour. I need to go shopping.'

A half-hour later, they pulled up outside Fourteen Apple Tree Drive. The large oak tree in the front garden now had a big hole in the side where Rick's car had crashed up against it. Tyre tracks had made a mess of the perfect green lawn. And her rose bush had been cleared away.

'Did you have something against that tree, Ms Capuletti?' Rufus asked.

'I wouldn't be surprised if you knew the number of times I fell from it as a kid, Rufus.'

He smiled at her and she thought it best not to test him on it.

'Thanks, Rufus, you've been very patient with me.'

'It has been my pleasure. I'll see you again tomorrow, Ms Capuletti.'

She tried to tip him but he refused, merely wishing her good luck with a tip of his cap and driving away.

So she was left standing on the suburban pavement of her old home—James's home—in her Dolce suit, make-up glamorous enough to outdo any movie star, and her heart on her sleeve.

She wheeled the brand-new BMX bike she had just bought up the driveway, eyes focused on nothing but the front door, until she found herself rapping on carved wood with an antique lion's head knocker that she had bought her father for his sixtieth birthday.

Voices on the other side of the door came closer until the door was opened. Matt, of the long grey ponytail stood staring at her.

'Well, if it isn't Siena Capuletti, sister of Rick Capuletti, defensive driver and one time inhabitant of this house.'

'Matt,' she said, her voice overly breathy. 'Hi. Is…is James about?'

As if he had come to the whisper of his

name, James backed around the far kitchen doorway, a tea-towel over his shoulder, in old jeans, a fitted blue polo shirt, endearingly torn at the collar, and bare feet, talking to someone he had left behind in the kitchen.

'James, you have another visitor,' Matt called out before fading into the next room.

James turned, saw her and stopped talking. His eyelids flickered, his mouth twitched, then all of a sudden, as though someone had flipped a switch on inside him, his whole face lit up.

He didn't even try to hide the fact that he had feelings for her. She had feelings right back. And that was all it took for her to know that she wasn't feeling torn up for nothing.

'Siena, hi,' James said, coming to her.

'Hi,' she said, feeling terribly small in the large open doorway. She shuffled from foot to foot. 'I have a present for Kane.' She motioned to the bike so obviously positioned by her legs.

His grey gaze trailed slowly to the bike via her red high heels, fancy suit and glamour make-up and she suddenly felt ridiculous. And the bike was so obviously only a ploy to get her to his side that it felt more like an albatross at her feet.

But when his gaze locked back on to her eyes, all feelings of ridiculousness just slipped away. The smile in his eyes was real. Utterly lovely. And important.

His hand rested against his heart. 'You look…amazing.' He reached out to take her by the tips of her fingers so he could look her over again. Then his smile slipped ever so slightly as he asked, 'Your interview—you've been?'

She nodded, her mouth dry as she found herself melting under his tender gaze. It had been so very long since she had known tenderness, if ever. The true warmth of a human touch, being looked upon as if she was something precious; it really was addictive.

'I know Kane is at school still, but I thought I should drop this off while I had the means to do so. The limo Max sent for me was huge. It seemed a waste not to take advantage.'

'You shouldn't have,' he said.

'Yeah. I should,' she returned and she

wondered if they were both talking about something other than the bike.

'Right. Then come in. Please.' He took the bike and leant it against the wall in the entranceway, and then he took a grip on her hand, tugging at her. Siena felt his thick calluses rubbing against her soft palm and she had to suppress a shiver.

She heard a woman's laugh ring out from the kitchen and hesitated.

'No, really it's okay,' she said. 'I shouldn't have come without calling. I don't know what I was thinking.'

Well, she had been thinking of him, and he would have to be as thick as a plank not to know it. And James was anything but thick. The moment he had seen her he'd known; he was just too much of a gentleman to gloat.

'Rubbish, and it doesn't matter,' James said to both of her statements, and he stepped through the doorway to join her outside so that they were within inches of one another beneath the trellis.

Siena was suddenly reminded of her first kiss

with…what was his name? Some boy she had dragged home for just that reason in the hope that Rick would find her and blow his top so that she could triumph like a right little teenager. She and what's-his-name had kissed. It had been all too brief and nicer than she had expected; Rick had been none the wiser and she had spent the next month catching a different bus home from school to avoid the poor guy.

She'd never been good at commitment, even then.

'Siena.' James's deep voice washed over her and she gazed up into his heavenly grey eyes. 'There is plenty of food and they are old friends whom I would love you to meet, so please come in. Join us.'

He twirled her hand until it hooked into his elbow, a place it was fast becoming used to, and he drew her inside.

She slipped off her shoes outside as though she had done it a hundred times before and, suddenly feeling small and delicate next to his strong, towering form, she followed where he led.

When the door shut behind her, the voices in

the kitchen stopped and two unfamiliar faces popped around the corner of the kitchen wall.

'Dave, Cate, this is Siena.'

Cate's eyes glinted. 'Aah. Kane's princess in shining armour.'

'Who?' Dave whispered.

'The one with the green car and the green eyes, who cleaned up his scrape,' Cate said through her teeth while coming forward and holding out her hand.

James released Siena from his secure grip and she found herself swept up in the tide as Cate drew her outside to where the gang had a barbecue heating up.

During the afternoon Siena allowed herself to see what it might feel like to be a part of James's world, a world of car-pooling, soccer fixtures, school PTA meetings and even dreaded piano lessons.

Considering her PDA was filled with the names of dry cleaners, pedicurists and cab companies around the world, she found herself floundering to join in. But then she would catch James looking at her with an affectionate smile lingering deep within his eyes, or he would lean across her as an excuse to rub his arm against hers, and the suburban world beneath her feet would solidify once more.

As the afternoon heated up, Siena had ditched her jacket in favour of her cream lace camisole and skirt. While Dave and Matt fought over the barbecue tongs, and Cate sat on the edge of the pool dangling her feet into the cool depths, she and James found themselves alone at the long wooden outdoor table, cool in the shade of the pergola.

She took a long drag of a Corona, relishing the lick of lemon at the end of each sip.

'Beer never tastes better than when it is drunk on a hot summer's day in the tropics,' James said, mirroring her thoughts exactly.

'Who are they?' she asked, watching as Cate flicked pool water over her husband's bare legs.

'Old friends. From when we were kids. I haven't seen them in months. Entirely my fault. I'm just lucky that they were stubborn enough to come a-knocking after all this time. It seems this weekend is a lucky one for me all around.'

Siena took a deep breath through her nose and slowly, slowly eked the bubbles of beer down her tight throat.

'So tell me about your interview,' James said, saving her from commenting. He straddled the bench seat so that he was facing her, and she felt the whole world fade away until there was no one else of import bar her and him.

Images of Max and his white satin trousers and ridiculous house swam to the fore, but she knew that wasn't what he wanted to know. Heck, he'd probably been there more times than she had.

So she bit the bullet and answered the question he was really asking.

'He offered me Rome,' she said.

James felt as though his legs had been kicked out from under him and if he hadn't been sitting he would have been in trouble. So much for this being his lucky weekend.

'Rome, eh?'

Siena nodded, biting at her inner lip in that way that gave him ideas.

The words *don't go!* fought to escape from

behind his clenched teeth. But that wasn't his place. He barely knew her. She barely knew him. What right did he have to tell her what to do? Or even to ask her? Especially when she had that stubborn look in her eye that told him that if anybody told her what to do she would be out of there as fast as the words left his mouth.

'That's what you wanted, right?' he asked, amazed he could even say the words.

She blinked, her brow furrowing. 'It was. It is. But still I asked him to give me time to think on it. He gave me twenty-four hours. So, by this time tomorrow, my fate will be sealed one way or the other.'

And like that, the pieces of the puzzle fell into place. She had come straight from the interview to him. Not to the mechanic shop. Not to Rick's house. And not to the airport.

This time *she* had come to *him*.

Suddenly this wasn't all conjecture any more. This wasn't a slow awakening by a beautiful woman who made him feel again. This had nothing to with any steps he had to take, twelve or otherwise.

Something big was happening between them. Both of them. Something unexpected and life-changing.

'Dude,' Matt called out, walking to James with the phone in his hand. James hadn't even heard it ring. He was used to being so attuned to it just in case it was Kane or—

'It's the school. Kane needs you.'

James was on his feet and running before Matt had finished talking. At the kitchen door he turned to Dave and Cate. 'Stay if you like. Have a swim. Eat. The school's not far. We'll be home soon.'

Dave and Cate waved him away. 'No, mate,' Dave said. 'It's time we left too.'

He shifted his gaze to find Siena sitting primly on the corner of his old outdoor bench, looking so beautiful, so elegant, so worried, and so real. Despite all the 'what ifs' rocketing through his mind, he wasn't finished with her yet.

'Come,' he said, holding out a hand.

And his heart clenched in his chest at the light that shone in her eyes at his simple request.

When she stood and came to him he knew

that he had no choice. By the end of that day he would be asking her to stay.

James drove to Kane's school and, though he kept to the speed limit the whole way, Siena still felt tension behind every gear change.

He looked across at her every moment that he could, and the smile in his eyes made her melt, but the moment he looked ahead his attention was focused on getting to Kane, and it made Siena wish she hadn't come along for the ride.

His first priority would always be his son and every minute she sat in the car only rubbed it in deeper.

They pulled up in front of the school and James even held the door open for her, taking her hand in his as he loped up the school steps. He moved slowly enough for her to keep up in her pencil skirt and high heels, but he jogged all the same.

Siena passed classrooms filled with kids at multicoloured desks positioned not in alphabetical rows as she had known but in circles, or with no desks at all as kids sat with their teachers on the floor. Again she felt the winds of change that had swept through the place since she'd left.

A woman about James's age, wearing a neat navy suit, with her long blonde hair pulled into a tight high ponytail, met them in the empty hall. James's hand slipped out of Siena's as he rushed to the blonde's side.

'James, I'm so sorry to have called you, especially with the school day almost over,' she said, laying a hand on James's upper arm.

Siena felt overwhelmingly proprietorial. Nothing that belonged to her gave her such a sense of ownership. Heck, her foreign sky girl friends who crashed at her apartment in Melbourne spent more nights in her bed than she did.

'Don't sweat it, Mandy. Really,' James said. 'You know the deal. If he needs me I'll be here. No matter what.'

Naturally Mandy chose that moment to notice Siena standing there looking like a wallflower at a school dance. She felt herself blushing as it slowly dawned on the teacher's pretty face that *she* had been James's 'no matter what'.

'Hi. I'm Siena. A friend of the family,' Siena said when James didn't.

She held out her hand and Mandy had to let go of James to take it. Siena had to fight back a victorious smile.

'Nice to meet you, Siena. Kane mentioned you in show and tell today.'

'Oh, my. What did he show?' she asked.

'His scar,' Mandy said, pinning Siena with that scary teacher stare they learned at university. 'Pretty impressive. Now, shall I take you to him?'

Mandy looked from James to Siena and back again.

'Go,' Siena said before James could tear himself apart any more. 'I'll be fine out here.'

She found a row of bright orange plastic chairs against the wall and sat down to wait.

'Thanks, Siena,' he said. 'We won't be long.'

He turned and walked into the small room with Mandy, their heads bent together as they went to help his son.

Siena spent several minutes in the too small chair, listening to James's deep voice murmuring through the open door. He spoke to his son, consoled him, and eventually joked with him, no doubt making Kane feel as though no matter what his world was secure.

She'd never felt so secure as a kid. She'd felt as if every day someone important in her life would leave her, as her mother had. And the day her father had died had only proved it to her. And both times it had been all her fault.

There was no way she wanted to bring that sort of negative energy to James and Kane. Imagine if she stayed, and in turn Kane turned out like her. Climbing out his bedroom window to meet his friends after curfew. Backchatting. One day leaving James and threatening never to return—

'It wasn't only Kane who mentioned you to me today.'

Siena turned to find Mandy leaning against the doorjamb. 'Oh?' Siena said.

'Matt did too.'

'You know Matt?' How well integrated in James and Kane's life was this woman?

Mandy sidled over and sat next to Siena,

crossing her legs neatly at the ankle. She smelled of chalk dust and juice. Compared with her delicate prettiness, Siena felt dark and dangerous to know. She felt the way she had felt at school around the happy-go-lucky kids with two parents and not a care in the world. She felt different. An outsider. Bad.

'I was the one who put James on to Matt,' Mandy said, 'and vice versa. I'm pretty proud of my matchmaking skills. They were made for each other.'

Siena noticed Mandy had blushed as she said Matt's name, her skin going pale and pink all at once.

'Are you and Matt…an item?' she asked, hoping her relief was not as obvious as it sounded to her ears.

'We have our moments,' Mandy said, her eyes going faraway and puppy dog soft for a few moments before she shook herself back to reality. 'Though I'm rather afraid I have more moments than he does.'

Well, there you go, Siena thought, shifting higher on her seat.

'So I take it you've become rather friendly with James over the past couple of days,' Mandy said, her ingenuous gaze shifting back to Siena.

'Considering how we met, he's been terribly kind to me,' Siena said, hedging her bets.

'I don't doubt it. He's a gentleman, which is why we in the community have all invested a lot of time in him and Kane. We are all as hopeful that they pull through with flying colours as they are. There is just so much potential in them both. Kane is such a good kid. Loyal. Polite. Smart as a tack. And then there's James…'

Mandy gave a small sigh and Siena again found herself wanting to claw the woman's pretty blue eyes out of her head.

'James really is the catch of the PTA,' Mandy continued. 'Half the single mums are madly in love with him and the other half want to take him home and feed him. Only he has no idea.'

Siena nodded along politely. But she had no intention of taking James home to feed him. Her idea of a home-cooked meal was a cab fare and a menu. How did a woman turn out that way? With not a nurturing bone in her body, and with no lifelong dream to marry, no desire to have kids, no wish to fall in love?

But, if she was all that, what was *she* doing mooning after James Dillon like it seemed the entire generation of single women who had come into his sphere did?

Either way, she had no intention of declaring James taken. And she had no intention of declaring herself immune. So she did her 'welcome aboard' smile, the one she had perfected to cope with exhausting overtime runs, and left Mandy to fill the silence if she so desired.

'Siena?'

Siena turned to find James, stormy-faced, with Kane skulking red-eyed behind him, and she was darned glad she had kept her mouth shut.

'It's time to go,' James said.

'Rightio.' Siena stood. 'Hey Kane-o. How're you going?'

Kane merely blinked at her as though he had never seen her before and slid further behind James's leg.

Good one, Siena. Kane-o feels awful. He didn't need to say a word for her to see he wasn't happy. And he sure had no reason to tell *her* about it. Who was she to him?

To *Kane-o* she was probably just some other fun grown-up who would swim in and out of his life with as much momentary niceness as a cute young girl who gave him a wink at the checkout at the supermarket. And she had gone and bought him a new bike like some kindly friend. Idiot!

She wiped her overly hot hands down the sides of her skirt.

'So we're off?' she asked, backing away towards the front door. Suddenly she *so* wanted to be off. Off and away. Far away.

It was suddenly so obvious. Her flight through life was *meant* to be a solo one with shifting rosters and impermanent friends. She had proved that by being poison to her own family. She had proved that by flourishing in a job that left no room for anyone stable in her life. And, right at that moment, she felt it in every itching nerve-ending, in every suffocating thought, and in every instinctive urge to run and keep on running.

'Yeah, it's time to go. See you, Mandy,' James said, leaning in to kiss her on the cheek. Though he kept his eyes on Siena the whole time, his brow furrowing as she twitched and switched feet and bit at her inner lip. 'Thanks for calling.'

'No worries.' Mandy got down on to her haunches so that she was on eye level with Kane, her slim arms resting neatly atop her knees. 'Feeling better now, kiddo?'

Kane nodded and gave a great dramatic sniffle.

'Well, you take care this weekend as Monday is project day and you don't want to miss that, do you?'

Kane thought about it for a second before nodding just once. Smart kid was keeping his options open too. Ha! It seemed the kid had some pretty strong similarities to her too if she went looking for them. But, unlike James, she had no reason to go looking for them. No reason at all.

She was a fly-by-the-seat-of-her-pants gal. She'd winged it her whole adult life, living day by day on ambition and gut instinct.

Attachments were for those who had others in their life who needed to be considered in the mix. And she had nobody.

James rubbed a hand over Kane's head and joined Siena. There was no holding hands this time and she wasn't sure if he was reading her signals or if, after his time with Kane, he was sending her some pretty strong ones of his own.

CHAPTER EIGHT

THE drive home was quiet.

James could have kicked himself for dragging Siena into such a domestic scene.

Siena was a jetsetter, a big city girl; she had been offered a dream job living in Rome, for goodness' sake, and there he was showing off the great bits of his life—Coronas in the sun, afternoon barbecues, the kind of relaxed suburban lifestyle that could be found nowhere else like they did it in the tropics.

And, in his extended selfishness of not wanting to let her out of his sight, he had gone and dragged her into…well, real life.

When they reached the house Matt's little red car was still outside but the others had gone. Kane was out of the car and in the house using the spare key from his backpack before James had even closed his car door.

Siena exited the car slowly as well. She shot him a straight smile.

'Why don't you come in and show Kane his new bike?' he suggested before she had the chance to speak.

'You show him,' she said, flapping a hand across her face.

He reached out and took her by the hand, having no intention of leaving their great day together on such an awkward note. 'Nope,' he said. 'Uh-uh. It's your gift. You have to give it to him.'

Her hand curled inside his until it moulded into a perfect fit. She blinked up at him and he wondered if she thought it was too. Whatever she was thinking, behind her ocean-green eyes she smiled and with a short nod gave into his tug and followed him inside.

'Kane, afternoon tea's on now if you want it. Reheated barbecue sausages,' he called once they were inside. 'Reheated anything is his favourite meal so if he doesn't come down within thirty seconds then I'll know for sure he's really ill.'

He waved through the kitchen window to Matt, who was scooping leaves out of the pool.

'You think he might be faking it?' Siena asked, delicately extricating her hand from his so she could head around to the safe side of the kitchen island. She leant her chin on her upturned palms and stared decidedly at some spot on the granite bench top.

Yep, she had definitely moved away from him again. Dammit.

She had held up her end, chatting with Mandy, knowing when to leave him alone, and reintroducing herself to his son. But they had let her down. He and Kane and the melancholic schtick they'd had going on for so long he couldn't remember what life was like before.

Well, he would just have to reel her back in and fast. He reached in the fridge for a plate of sausages he knew Matt would have left for them. He put them in the microwave, pressed the reheat button—every single dad's favourite technologi-cal advance—and pulled up a barstool.

'I don't rightly know,' he admitted. 'He pulls stunts like this all the time, and I've let him. But today it just felt wrong, like I was giving into him rather than parenting him, and I told him as much at the school, hence the huff upstairs.'

Siena smiled though it didn't reach her eyes. Of course it didn't. This woman was happiest spending her days with pilots and businessmen and first class travellers, not sick kids and their clueless fathers.

'Were you a huffer?' he asked, doing his best to include her, to remind her that they were at least of the same species even if not of the same life experience.

'As a kid?' she asked. And, when he nodded, 'Sure. World class. I was born twelve years after Rick, so it was inevitable that I become a pampered princess or a huffer. There was no way on God's green earth that Rick would have allowed the former, and Dad was so busy working, as he thought that was the best way to provide for us after Mum was gone, to sway the balance.'

'Sounds like they both deserved all they got.'

James had meant it as a joke, but the second the words left his mouth Siena's face turned pale as paper. Then he remembered that her father had died when she was a teenager. Something in the way she had talked about it made him sure she thought herself to blame.

He'd been there. Losing the person you love the most and knowing deep down that there must have been something you could have done to stop it...

'Hey, I didn't mean anything by that,' he said, reaching for her hand, but she pulled it away.

'I know. It's okay. Really.'

The microwave pinged, telling them the sausages were cooked. James got off his seat and rapped on the window to tell Matt food was on. Matt waved him outside.

'I won't be a sec,' he told Siena, hesitating before leaving her with her thoughts.

The moment James left the room, Siena let her head fall until it hit the kitchen bench. Oversensitive, much? While seated thus, she heard a shuffle of sneakers on tile as Kane skulked in.

Excellent. Now, after their awkward meeting at the school, she had no idea what to say to the kid.

Should she laugh along with him that he'd got out of school early? Heck, she'd done so enough times to know a pro when she saw one. Or ought she lean down on her knees like Mandy until she was at his eye level and ask if he was feeling better? Well, *that* just gave her the heebie-jeebies. If anyone had baby-talked to her at Kane's age she would have thought them imbeciles.

Kids were little people. They were no more stupid or ignorant than many adults she knew. So the only thing she could do with Kane was be herself.

'So, do you want a sausage on bread or are you still feeling too rotten?' she asked.

Kane watched her from beneath long dark lashes, his mouth twisting as he thought about it. She wasn't sweet like Mandy. She wasn't laid-back like Matt. And she wasn't blinded by love like his dad. She shot him two raised eyebrows to show she was not one to be messed with.

'So, what's it to be, Kane-o? Tea or sympathy? As I see it, you've worked yourself into a corner so you can't have both.'

He blinked, surprised at having been spoken to like that. Then he squared his small shoulders and moved around her to the bread box. He pulled out a loaf and a breadboard and set to plying a heap with tomato sauce and butter.

Well, there you go, Siena thought, more shocked that her bluff had worked than Kane had been at being bluffed. A glimmer of hope sprang from deep within her, like a ray of light at the bottom of a well.

'Do you like mayonnaise?' Kane asked without looking at her. 'I hate it but Dad always has mayonnaise on his sausages.'

'No, thanks,' Siena said, moving to stand by Kane, bringing a spare knife from the cutlery drawer for use in the mayo jar. 'Bread, butter and tomato sauce only for me. Anything else is just not Australian.'

Kane looked up at her with a small smile. He still looked tired, his eyes were still pink, but there was definite attitude behind that smile. The attitude was definitely not James and she wondered if he had inherited that along with his brown eyes from his mother.

'Do you want to see my room now?' Kane asked and, buoyed by the hope radiating from within her, Siena actually said yes.

Kane grabbed a rolled up sausage in bread for himself, took a hold of her right hand in his sticky one and dragged her upstairs.

Halfway up the stairs Siena's confidence failed her as memories swarmed in. Okay, so the demon she'd thought she'd kicked had been bruised, but it was still alive and kicking. She paid close attention to the differences since the last time she had been upstairs several years before.

The stairs had been carpeted in her time; now they were polished wood. The stair rail had been replaced, the polish and grain re-minding her of the work in James's workshop. She let her left hand trail along the wood, feeling the craftsmanship, imagining James putting long hours into the piece to make sure the quality was up to his exacting standards.

But, even with James's stamp all over it, it was still the same staircase. She could have traversed the walk with her eyes closed.

The hairs on the back of Siena's neck stood on end as she prepared herself to face the whisper of old ghosts she had been running from for years. The fights with her brother after her many teenage tantrums, the accusations that her behaviour was putting undue stress on her father's poor heart, the day her father died…

Kane turned left at the top of the stairs. Some of the anxiety subsided as she saw that Rick's room had been turned into a kind of games area for Kane. She'd have to tell him that, to be sure.

Kane continued dragging her into what had once been her old room. Her pink floral wallpaper, white lace curtains and posters of Nirvana and Pearl Jam had been replaced by plain yellow walls, heavy white curtains and Kane's favourite toys, including a football signed by the North Queensland Cowboys. But even as Kane pointed out his computer, his stereo and other prized possessions, Siena's eyes kept flickering to the half-open door at the other end of the hall.

The master bedroom.

No doubt now James's bedroom.

Her dad's old bedroom…

She hadn't meant to be home.

She had gone AWOL from school. It had been swimming that day and she had forgotten her togs, so rather than get in trouble she had forged a sick note from her dad and had played truant.

After a day spent at the local video game arcade, she had bought herself an ice-block with her bus money and had spent an hour walking home.

She'd let herself in just before one o'clock,

She'd clomped up the stairs and headed into her dad's room looking for any spare change he might have left on his chest of drawers.

And she had found him there, on his bed, not breathing…

Her mouth suddenly went dry. And it was only when Kane called out to her that she realised she was at the end of the hall with her hand on the doorknob.

'Siena!' James called out when he and Matt made it back into the kitchen. His voice grew more insistent when there was no response, 'Kane?'

'You check upstairs and I'll check out front,' Matt suggested.

James took the stairs two at a time, hoping against hope he would find both of them there, though considering the way Siena had looked upon Kane like an alien the last time they had been together he wasn't all that hopeful.

Buying a new toy for Kane or teaching him a new trick each time she came over wouldn't endear Kane to her for ever. And he wasn't entirely sure she had a clue of any other way to make a connection with him. But he wanted her to know he was more than willing to help her if she was willing to learn.

But was he only being selfish? Following

his own desires with such blind abandon and not thinking through Kane's wishes and welfare?

Or did Kane long for a new mother as James longed for Siena? With a blind reaching hope that one day it would all work out for him?

Please don't be gone, he thought, *please don't be gone*. If she'd done a runner... He didn't even want to go there.

He slowed when he heard a murmur of voices coming from inside his bedroom of all places.

'My dad made this one before I was born,' he heard Kane say.

'It's beautiful,' he heard Siena say, and his knees all but collapsed beneath him. He was overwhelmed by the relief flowing through his veins.

'Dad didn't make this one. It was Mum's. She liked things a little flashier than Dad and I like. We like the classics.'

James leant back against the hallway wall and bit back a smile. What a funny kid...

'What's *your* mum like?' Kane asked, out of the blue, and James's smile slipped.

He almost decided to burst in to save Siena from answering that question but he knew he had to let this play itself out. Kane had brought it up. Kane was the one asking questions and talking about Dinah. And Kane had never once done that off his own bat with anyone bar James in the year since his mother's death.

'I never knew my mother,' Siena said, her voice now a little quieter so James had to strain his ears to hear. He listened so hard his head hurt. 'She died when I was born.'

'Bummer,' Kane whispered in some kind of awe that someone else he knew had lost their mother too.

'My thoughts exactly,' Siena said.

James was disappointed to think that might be the end of it until she said, 'I wish I could have known her. Even for just a little while.'

Her voice was even, but he heard a creak of bed-springs and he knew she'd had to sit down. On his bed. Siena Capuletti was right now on his bed. How the heck *had* they ended up in his bedroom of all places? His mouth twitched as he pictured her snooping and Kane catching her out. If that was how it had happened, maybe he was in luck after all...

'You're lucky, Kane-o,' she said.

'*I* am?' Kane asked. 'But—'

'Uh-uh,' she said cutting him off. 'No buts about it. You know what your mother looked like outside of photographs. How she laughed. What her favourite food was. What time she liked to get up in the morning. The type of furniture she liked, even. Right?'

Kane sighed and said, 'Yeah, I do.'

'And, besides all of that, you have a truly great dad. A dad who loves you so much that he would leave a perfectly nice barbecue lunch with sausages, and steak even, to pick you up early from school.'

'You think my dad's great?' Kane asked, and James held his breath for longer than was probably healthy.

'I do, Kane.' She paused, and then said, 'I think your dad is the greatest man I have ever met.'

James let out his breath nice and slowly. *The greatest man.* She hadn't said the greatest dad, but the greatest man. Oh, boy.

'Heck, Kane-o, I reckon to have a dad like that you are spoilt rotten.'

There was a small silence before the bed-springs creaked a little more and James imagined his son climbing up on to his bed beside the woman who had so quickly moved into his own heart.

Come on, Kane, he wished as hard as he could. *Do right by the both of us, kiddo. Show her we Dillon boys are worth sticking around for.*

'She hated mornings,' Kane finally said. 'Dad was on morning patrol to get me ready for school but she was a night owl, so she always lay beside me on the bed until I fell asleep at night. I sometimes wake up thinking she'll be there…'

More squeaking bed-springs. What was going on? James risked a peek through the slit of the doorway but he could only make out their legs—Kane's skinny with knobbly knees below his school shorts, and Siena's shapely, tanned, barefoot with hot red toenails and crossed neatly at the knee.

'The last thing our mums would want is for us to be sad, Kane. Don't you think yours would want you to be doing well in your school projects? And making friends in class? And smiling all the time like you do when you're on your trampoline?'

'I guess.'

'And I think your dad would want that for you too. You must know that's what he wants most in the whole world, for you to be happy.'

'I know.'

'So, be happy.'

'Just like that?'

'Just like that. Wake up, whack a smile on your face and aim to have a good day every day. It's that simple.' After a pause she added, 'Okay, so it's not that simple. But it's a good start, right? And I think we would both do well to remember that a little more.'

Kane's legs leant sideways, into Siena, and her legs instantly uncrossed and went knock-kneed and askew. James realised that Kane had hugged her. He put a hand against the wall to steady himself.

'Right, okay,' Siena said, her voice suddenly thick. 'We'd better get downstairs or your dad will think we've run away and he might then eat all the sausages himself.'

James pushed himself away from the wall and ran down two stairs and waited for Kane to barrel out the door before taking a step back up.

'Dad!' Kane called, his eyes bright and lit by an inner fire that made James glow from the inside out.

'Yes, buddy?' he said, doing his best not to take the kid in his arms and hug him tight.

'I left my hot dog in my room.' And Kane ran off as if the wind was at his heels.

Siena came out of his room, her mouth falling into a shocked 'O' as she saw him at the top of the stairs. She glanced back into the room behind her.

'Don't tell me, Kane was showing off the camphor blanket box. He loves that piece. When he was younger and loved playing hide and seek he could be found there nine times out of ten. He smelled like camphor until he was five.'

She smiled at him, her eyes bright and her cheeks pink. 'Yep. That was it. Now, where are those hot dogs? I'm starved.'

She slid past him, leaving behind a trail of expensive perfume, heat and bashfulness as she jogged down the stairs.

After the strangest afternoon tea date of her life, eating reheated sausages over the kitchen sink with a guy, a kid and an ageing hippy, Siena said her goodbyes.

'Is that your bike at the front door?' Kane asked, as they walked straight past it.

'Oh, heck, I almost forgot! I bought it for you,' Siena said. 'Considering I squished your last one, I thought it was only fair. But you are only allowed to ride it if you tell your dad every time and you always wear your helmet and pads. And wake up every day how we talked about, deal?'

'Wow! Sure. Thanks,' Kane gushed, taking it in his hands and spinning the handle bars and testing the bell. 'I promise!'

'Say goodbye,' James told his son.

'Goodbye, Siena!' Though Kane was gone to them now, running the bike round and round the lounge.

'What was that all about?' he asked, walking her to his car as she hadn't been able to convince him he had no need to drive her home. 'Waking up every day?'

She leant against the passenger door of his dark sedan and crossed her arms. 'Nothing important,' she said, more than glad he hadn't come looking for them any earlier than he had.

He sauntered over and leant against the car beside her, mirroring her stance, folding his arms and half-smiling back.

'So?' he said.

'So,' she repeated, willing herself not to blush beneath the warmth of his gaze, 'this afternoon has been…educational.'

James watched her but she had no idea what he was thinking. She had barely known him long enough to be able to read his verbal language much less his body language. Though, for some reason, all through the sausages and bread he'd been acting like the cat who'd caught the canary.

It had left her feathers feeling ruffled. That decisiveness, that straight stare, the constant half-smile—she found that side of him utterly sexy. Strong. Masculine. And attractive as hell. And she too hadn't been able to keep her own smile off her face all afternoon.

Though she thought that the conversation with Kane had had as much to do with her unbelievably high spirits as anything else.

There she had been, in her father's old room, the place in which the hardest memories of her short life had taken place, and she had been stronger than she had ever thought herself able to be. She'd had to be, for there had been someone else in that room who had needed her to be.

'You could stay,' James said, and Siena was torn from her heroic daydreams.

She waited for him to finish his sentence and, in the silent moment that stretched on, she thought perhaps that was all he was planning to say and her heart swelled. Literally. She could feel it filling her chest until she could barely breathe.

But, after a pause, he added, 'For dinner.' And her expectant heart deflated back to its regular below average size.

'Nah,' she said. 'I don't think so. It's my last night here and I really ought to spend some time with Rick's family. Especially since I don't know when I'll be back again. If I do take the Rome gig it might be a while. A really long while.'

Not in the least put off by her assertion, a flicker of warmth lit his eyes and then he reached out and tucked a stray curl behind her ear. Siena could not stop the ragged sigh from escaping her lips.

'So why not stay?' he repeated, his deep voice gentle and personal and completely distracting. And this time Siena was in no doubt there would be no qualifier to his statement.

He was suggesting she *stay*, stay. In Cairns. For him.

Siena felt breathless and full of oxygen all at once. But, before she had the chance to frame a thought, much less a response, James leaned across and kissed her.

In the split second before their lips met, Siena half-expected James's kiss to be timid and wary. Sheepish, even. So far as she knew, she was the first woman he had kissed since meeting his wife several years before.

But when their lips at long last touched, his were warm, determined and sure. He knew exactly what he was doing. And Siena ended up the one who felt nothing but shaky.

Her body wilted against the hot car.

Her eyes drifted closed.

Pretty soon she felt more than just shaky. Pretty soon, as his kiss deepened, as she realised that there was nothing in the least bit carefree and unprompted about it, she felt tender, fluttery, adored and cherished and as though a fire had been lit beneath her toes.

She felt more alive and more scared than ever before. She felt as if she had stepped into a lift shaft to find the lift was in fact not there. She was in free fall, but she knew that James would be there to catch her in the end with his strong, creative hands.

Though neither of them moved from their

position side by side, their arms crossed, a foot between her warm melting body and his, Siena had never felt more intimate with a man.

James was communicating so much tenderness and hope and effortless sensuality to her that every last concern she had about him, about home, about family, about love, melted away. She wished with all her might that those creative hands were on her. Touching her. Teaching her. Holding her.

Nothing mattered in that moment but James. James's lips. James's warmth. James's strength compared with her own mounting weakness. James's desire for her to stay—despite her inexperienced heart and despite what she had thought had been an all-consuming love for his son.

As though he had heard the thought echoing in her cotton wool filled mind, James pulled away.

Siena leant towards him, continuing the kiss as long as possible.

She sighed in disappointment as his lips finally left hers. Her unusually heavy eyes flickered open, expecting to see some semblance of guilt or surprise in James's eyes.

But he was simply smiling. Really smiling. His grey-blue eyes were jewel-bright. His mouth kicked open to show a set of neat white teeth which would do just fine in any toothpaste commercial. And the crease in his right cheek that had threatened to show itself again and again now came out in full force. It was as though he finally had something private and wonderful in his life worth smiling about.

Siena could do nothing but stare. This was one beautiful man. A man with a heartbreakingly handsome face, with bottomless soulful eyes, with a huge capacity to give, who filled out a pair of old jeans just right, who liked her. There was absolutely no doubting it now. He really, really liked her.

And silly, selfish her; she had gone and done exactly the opposite of what she had promised herself. When all the while she had been thinking of him, and while she hadn't been paying attention to her own feelings, she had gone and fallen slap bang in love with the guy.

The thought landed with a thud at the base of her skull, and where before she had felt on top of the world, she suddenly felt numb from head to toe.

'Dare I ask what is going on behind those stormy eyes of yours?' he asked, his gorgeous smile still so devastatingly in place.

He uncrossed his arms to reach out and run his knuckles along her cheek. Her skin heated under his touch, leaving a trail of fire across her face.

'I'm thinking you ought to call me a cab,' she said, making sure there was no inflection at the end of her sentence. No question. She had to go. And fast.

A cab would be quicker than Rufus, and less likely to ask pertinent questions.

'You're a cab,' he said, not letting her off the hook that easily.

A strange movement caught her attention out of the corner of her eye. Siena looked up at the first floor to find the heavy white curtains in her old bedroom flapping back and forth.

They had an audience.

Oh, great. How long had Kane been watching them? It had felt so good to be able to help someone who reminded her of herself as a kid stay on the right track. The very last thing she wanted was to be the one to send Kane into confusion, spiralling him further off course.

'Siena, don't do this. Don't run—' James began.

Siena cut him off before he said anything either of them would regret.

'James. I *really* think you ought to call a cab.' She gestured towards the window and, like a moth to a flame, his eyes sought out his son, who now had his nose and palms pressed against the window.

James's brow furrowed, his smile waned and his jaw set hard and tight as he reconciled how much he wanted her with the fact that Kane may have seen it all.

'Right,' he said, his voice barely above a whisper. 'I can drop you home…'

'Stay here. I'll be fine. But Kane needs you.'

And I don't. I love you, but I don't need *anybody!*

James nodded once. 'That he does.'

Siena reached into her handbag for her mobile phone and she called directory assistance for the number of a cab company. And this time James didn't try to stop her.

She tried a beaming smile on for size. But even she knew it didn't quite fit. Because she knew deep down that he loved Kane so much that he *would* let her go. There was too much to consider, and with James at her side, looking so stunning and smelling so good she just couldn't consider anything bar kissing him again.

As though the fates were sending her a sign, the cab arrived in record time to spirit her away, and James leant in the passenger seat window to wish her goodbye.

'I'll call you later,' he said.

I might not answer, she thought.

'Tell Kane I hope he's feeling better. And that he'd better stick to the footpath on that new bike of his.'

She turned to the cabbie and gave Rick's address.

'Goodbye, James,' she said as the cab pulled away from the kerb.

This time as she drove away she kept her eyes dead ahead.

CHAPTER NINE

AFTER taking a long cool early shower, during which she had thought herself in circles until she felt more confused than ever, Siena changed into her red velvet pyjamas and went downstairs to find Rick alone in his den, drinking a brandy and reading that morning's sports section.

'So why aren't you out with your young man?' he asked, not looking up.

'He's not my young man,' Siena said, realising she had perhaps been a bit too vehement when Rick looked at her in disbelief.

She regretted sitting down when he folded his paper.

'And why not?'

'Because I never have young men in my life. Not in the way that you mean. I…I can't.'

'Why can't you?'

'Because until recently I thought that relationship-wise I was little more use to any man than rat poison. And, though I'm not so sure that that's the case any more, I'm still feeling pretty raw.'

She stared at her fingernails, cleaning out an imaginary speck of dirt.

'I had a conversation with an eight-year-old this afternoon that made me realise how ridiculous it was that I have always blamed myself that Dad died that day.'

'You *what?*' Rick practically exploded on the spot, his newspaper rustling as it half fell to the floor in great flapping black and white sheets.

She glared at Rick, her thoughts, and memories, and emotions on high alert, all akimbo and mixed up and backwards since James had gone and kissed her and liked her and made her fall in love with him.

'Come on, Rick. The day he died, the day I played truant from school and came home early and found him on his bed, so cold and so still. You blustered in and yelled—and I quote—*"Now look what you have done"*. But it wasn't my fault, Rick,' she said, looking her big burly brother dead in the eye. 'It's taken a lot for me to realise that. But that won't make a lick of difference to my life unless I know that you realise it too.'

Rick opened his mouth to deny it. Siena let him take his time to gather himself. It had been some accusation after all. But then something inside him seemed to extinguish, leaving him looking every one of the twelve years older than her that he was.

'He was sixty-five,' Rick said. 'He'd had heart problems all his life. And I am an ass if I ever made you feel that way.'

Siena could do nothing but stare at her big brother as the words she had longed to hear all her life spilled from his lips.

But, rather than wanting to throw them back in his face with a great self-satisfied, I told you so, she just let them wind around her like a long coiling rope drawing her closer to the brother who, until that moment, she had always looked upon as an unfeeling tyrant.

'Dad died because he ate salami like it was going out of fashion,' he said, his voice raw and rough. 'He worked himself far too hard and never did a day's exercise in his life. I am truly sorry if I ever made you think any different.'

He sat back and ran a hand over his eyes.

'You were such a handful as a kid, Siena. You were so smart. So full of life. Hell, you still are. Yet you were throwing all that talent away on late nights with your friends and parties. And it pains me deep down that that's what you are still doing with your life.'

Her eyes burned and she rubbed at them frantically. Now was not the time to fall apart. This was too important. 'But I was only ever trying to get Dad to pay attention,' she said, her voice barely above a whisper.

And you, she thought. *I just wanted you to see me. To really see me, not just be angry with me. Not be disappointed…*

'I know,' Rick said, lifting his face to look her in the eye. 'I know. And I knew it then too. But you were his light. You were his everything.'

She knew it. Deep down she knew, though it had taken some convincing. But she also needed to know what she was to Rick too. Theirs had been the defining relationship of her childhood. This wasn't really ever about her father; it was about the father figure sitting before her.

'So why did *you* always tell me off if I wore mismatched socks, when he never once even lifted his voice if I came home an hour after curfew with smudged lipstick?'

'We all have our own ways of loving, *Piccolo*. Mine is more forward. Verbose. Dad's was to sit back and watch with wonder as his little girl grew into such a personality. He loved your energy and your spirit and chastised me daily for trying to clip your wings.'

'He did?' *That* she had never known.

'You have to remember I was twelve when you were born, *Piccolo*. Twelve when my mother died. Twelve when *you* became the apple of my hero's eye. You, who stayed out after curfew, who never tried in school, who pierced her belly at age fourteen and had a fake ID. And I was not much older than you are now when Dad died. Imagine yourself now, in the prime of your life, suddenly being lumbered with a teenager. When you become a parent, Siena, your own needs and wishes must come second.'

And, just like that, all of Siena's indignation melted away. It flowed from her mind and off her shoulders and out the tips of her fingers, leaving her feeling as if she had run a marathon.

She thought again of her conversation with Kane on James's bed, that small face looking up at her as though she had all knowledge of heaven and earth. And looking back at him all she'd wanted to do was protect him, keep him safe, do all she could to see that he was never hurt.

Be happy, she'd insisted to Kane. *Don't ride your bike without your helmet.*

That was all Rick had ever done for her. He'd spent his own young adulthood trying only to protect her. She swallowed, the taste of the words *I'm sorry too* burning hot on her tongue.

'Rick, I—'

'It's okay,' he said, pulling his hulking form from his chair. 'I know.'

As he passed, Rick kissed the top of her head, then left her alone, and she felt as if she had only just met him for the first time.

And as such she realised how much catching up she had to do and with so little time in which to do it.

After Kane had fallen asleep James sat slumped down into a sofa in the unlit lounge room. It was still sweltering hot and he could smell the scent of a coming storm on the air.

'I was thinking of having a quick cup of tea before I head off,' Matt said. 'Would you like one? Hot? Iced?'

James nodded. 'Whatever you're having, thanks, mate.'

Hot? Cold? It didn't really matter. It was all an excuse to get Matt to stay. He needed to talk. And somehow he knew that talking to his blog simply wouldn't cut it this time.

Over the last months his blog had been helpful in getting his feelings off his chest, but now he needed someone to talk back. He needed answers.

'You've got a whole new furrow in your brow that I haven't seen before and for a guy with as many furrows as you that's saying something,' Matt said once he had settled.

James grimaced. 'Furrows are distinguished, right?'

'Unfortunately the best *I* could hope for would be distinguished; on you they're just handsome.'

'You think?' James asked, the beginnings of a smile taking the tension from his forehead.

'Don't get me wrong, buddy. I wouldn't have a clue. I'm only repeating what I hear around the traps.'

'You been talking to Mandy again?'

Matt took a sip of his tea, but James saw the pink come and go in his friend's cheeks. 'Her, and others. Now, back to the subject at hand. I'm thinking this new furrow is all about the girl.'

'You'd be thinking right,' James said.

'Siena's into you, mate. That much is as obvious as the furrows on your handsome brow. Heck, even Mandy couldn't wait five minutes after you left the school today before ringing me to chastise me for not giving her the whole picture about her.'

He was *sure* Matt was on the money there. The way she'd watched him when she'd thought he wasn't looking. The way she'd found an excuse to spend time with him had been almost as feeble as the one he had found to spend time with her.

And then there was the way she had responded to his kiss. Her whole body had flickered to life, melting into him, her amazing energy wrapping itself about him like an electrical coil.

'I kissed her,' James admitted.

'Whoa.'

'I think Kane may have seen it.'

'Oh, boy.'

James leant forward, sinking his chin into his left palm, and ran hard fingers across his mouth. 'And I asked her to stay.'

'Man.' Matt breathed slowly out. 'I knew that you two were sparky together, but do you think you might be rushing this a little, buddy?'

'I don't have a choice. She came to town for a job interview. Her boss offered her a job in Rome. And tomorrow afternoon she has to give him her decision before flying home to Melbourne. I don't have the luxury of dating, wooing, taking my time.'

'She seems a right royal cracker of a girl, but are you sure she's as far along on this thing as you are?'

'I overheard her telling Kane that I am the greatest man she has ever known.'

Matt's expression showed he wasn't nearly as convinced by that statement as James had been.

'She didn't have to say that. She could have said any number of things; she could have said I was a cool dad or a nice guy, or cute as a button—she didn't have to use those exact words.'

'Is that all the evidence you have?'

'Matt, she makes me smile,' James said, letting it all out in a gush of words. 'She makes me *want* to smile just by being with her. Heck, she makes me smile even when I *don't* want to. Constantly. Every moment she is with me, nervous energy spilling from her until I too can't stop fidgeting, and every moment she isn't as I count down the moments until I can be with her again. Siena isn't just a beautiful woman who takes my breath away. She's my ray of hope.'

'Well, then…' Matt said, thinking on it very seriously.

'Well, then?' James repeated, desperate for his friend's take on the whole situation.

'Well, then, I don't think you need for me to tell you what to do. You seem pretty hell-bent on doing it anyway.'

James's shoulders tensed as he broached the one great stumbling block as he saw it. Distance didn't frighten him, nor her skittishness, nearly as much as how his son would take the news.

'What about Kane?'

'What about Kane?' Matt repeated, his eyes narrowing.

'Shouldn't he have some sort of say in all this?'

'In who gets invited to his birthday parties? Sure. In who gets to play on his trampoline? No doubt. But in who you love? Because I think you are trying to tell me that you love this woman.'

He glanced at James, who gave him one sure—certain—nod.

'Nope. Uh-uh. Kane doesn't have a say there. Not even you can have much of a say in that one, buddy. And, if you're looking for my take on all this, Kane could do with having such a cracker of a girl in his life nearly as much as you could.'

Matt tapped James on the knee, then gathered their empty iced tea glasses and headed into the kitchen, leaving James alone with his thoughts.

And the one thought that rose above all others was that when he had kissed Siena, she had kissed him right back.

It had moved him so much he had forgotten himself completely in her warm giving lips. He had forgotten all responsibilities bar kissing her until the end of time. And, when he had looked up and seen Kane at the window, he knew that his responsibilities had been blurred behind fear long enough.

Meeting Siena, knowing Siena, and, yes, loving Siena had only shone a bright big ray of North Queensland sunlight on what his responsibilities were.

To be happy.

For his son to be happy, well-adjusted, ready to be out in the world, he had to be happy first.

And to be happy he needed Siena.

He didn't want her to look him up in six months' time *if* she came back to visit her family. Contemplating six months between seeing her face, touching her hand, kissing her… His heart felt as if it was being ripped from his chest.

Talking it through with Matt, or writing down the multitude of conflicting feelings into his blog, wouldn't solve the problem. He knew that now.

Confronting the problem head-on would be the only way through.

'Matt, sorry to keep you so long again today. But I have a big favour to ask.'

Siena sat cross-legged on her bed reading her emails when she heard a knock at the front door.

Rick, Tina and the kids had gone out for their regular Friday night pasta at Tina's parents' place and Siena hadn't been kidding when she'd begged off with a headache. So she sat still and waited for the door-knocker to leave.

But, a few moments later, Siena heard it again. And this time she realised it wasn't a knock at the front door; it was a rap of pebbles against her bedroom window.

She hitched her pyjama bottoms higher and moved to the window, peering out to the moonlit suburban front garden to find James, standing in the middle of the yard with arms outstretched and a bunch of flowers in his hand with Rick's big stupid Triton fountain shooting water into the air behind him.

Her head hurt from thinking all afternoon, and she knew that she had a big night of thinking ahead of her still. Surely the last thing she needed was for James to make some great romantic gesture to cloud things.

But she could hardly shoo him away. He was out there with flowers, for goodness' sake!

Feeling like a character in a movie, she

pulled open the window and yelled out in a stage whisper. 'Stop throwing things or you'll break the glass! Stay right there. I'm coming down.'

She ran from her room, down the stairs two at a time and out on to the front lawn, the cool grass squishing beneath her feet. She only realised she was in her pyjamas when James's mouth dropped open.

'Jeez Louise.' He whistled, his eyes raking in the skimpy expanse of crushed red velvet and the crescent of exposed skin above the elastic of her trousers.

Doing her best to ignore the effect such a comment had on her libido, she stormed over to him, grabbed him by the bouquet-free hand and dragged him into the shadows of an over-hanging willow tree at the side of the house.

'What the hell do you think you are you doing?' Her lungs were tight with the extra work her pumping adrenalin was giving them.

She stared at the flowers—iceberg roses, at least a couple of dozen of them—though he wasn't quite suave enough to have given them to her in order to give her hands something to do other than poke him in the ribs, as she was doing now.

'When you left the house today you gave me the sense that you weren't coming back,' he said. 'And I don't think that I can let that happen.'

'Oh, you can't?' She crossed her arms, staving off the thrilling shivers that were running up and down her body at his words.

'I had planned to serenade you,' he said, his mouth kicking into that half-smile that had made her half crazy for him in the first place, 'if that was what it took to get you to see me, but it turns out you are easier than I had expected.'

Her hands dropped to her hips and she glared back at him. 'I'm *easy*?'

He grinned and her giddy heart all but went kaput.

'Easy? I don't think any man in the history of time has had to put as much work into wooing a woman as I have. It has been very demanding attempting to get you to realise how much I think of you.'

Her hands dropped to her sides and all her self-fuelled anger fled. 'You think of me?'

'Siena, sweetheart.' He took a step towards her. 'Since meeting you I've thought of little else.'

He moved in again, taking her by the arms so that the flowers squished up against her sides, the soft petals and sharp stems creating the strangest sensation against her skin. Or maybe it was his nearness that was giving her such new sensations. But when she glanced up into his warm grey eyes, all sensation was lost to her.

'James, I'm not all that special,' she said, trying to drag herself out of the whirlpool of affection in his eyes. 'Believe me. When one lives alone and has no responsibilities bar one's occupation, that person can't help but be fascinating to a person with the responsibility of the world on their shoulders.'

His smile deepened and she was all but undone. 'You've got me there. With a child in your life the term responsibility-free time becomes a pipe dream.'

She swallowed and managed to gather her thoughts. 'Are you really trying to sell that life to me, James? Because you really are making a hash of it.'

But he just shrugged. 'I've realised I can't sell it to you by having Kane butter you up, or plying you with beers in the sunshine, or taking you on long leisurely trips up to Kuranda. If this is meant to be I shouldn't have to sell it to you as some sort of alternative to the glamour of Rome. You should want it despite the inducements.'

'I like inducements,' she said, glancing at the roses he was waving about. But he didn't seem to get it. 'Oh, just give me the damn flowers.'

Siena reached out a hand, flapping her fingers against her palm to hurry him up. James handed them over. Once she had them, she couldn't help but bring the bouquet to her nose, burying her face in the familiar scent.

The roses weren't just any roses. They were his, cut from his own garden, and they smelled as good as the one she had kept by her bedside. They weren't glistening in fake dew like roses she had received from suitors before. They weren't wrapped in layers of fabulous tulle and ribbon. Some were bruised, others had lost petals. But to Siena they were the most beautiful gift she had ever received.

'They're beautiful, James.'

'Not nearly as beautiful as you.'

She could have laughed. It really had been some time since he had done this. But she couldn't. The tone of his voice told her how true he thought his words. It wasn't some line. It was a declaration.

But, after the topsy-turvy evening she'd had, a declaration was the last thing she was prepared to deal with. If she could somehow send him away until morning…

She looked up to find he was inches from her, the big bouquet the only thing between them. His grey eyes glittered in the moonlight, serious and intent, despite the banter he had kept up the whole time.

He was going to kiss her. Any moment now she was going to find herself enveloped in his warm, intimate embrace.

She swallowed down a sudden flash of trepidation. When she had left his house that day she had planned on not looking back, but that didn't make a lick of difference to her determination if James had every intention of remaining in her future.

But for her that future was still a big blur. For the first time in her life she really had to look ahead and not back to the past. And as yet it was undecided. She had no clue what she was going to tell Max tomorrow.

Rome was all she'd ever wanted and it was within reach. But now she wasn't entirely sure she wanted Rome for the right reasons. Had it been because it was her one great chance to live the life she really desired above all others? Or had it been because she wanted to prove herself to Rick? All these years she had defined herself by his opinion of her and now that had been turned on its head.

And then there was James…

She needed time to sort through everything she had learned about herself and the men in her life over the last couple of days. If James had simply not come, if he'd let her be for the night, who knew what decision she might have come to in the morning?

But in that moment all she knew was that she needed just a little more time…

His eyes lost all trace of a glimmer as he began to bend his mouth to hers, and the only words she could think of to stall him came out in a great rush.

'James, I've been reading your blog.'

She had thought he had been hard to read, but in that moment she realised she had come to know that face so well over the last couple of days.

The tightening in his right cheek was a dead giveaway that he was affected. And the fact that the kiss that had been threatening did not eventuate was a pretty good giveaway too.

'I saw it on the computer in your workshop that first day,' she admitted. 'And that night, after knowing about your wife, after you told me yourself about Dinah, I had to know everything. I couldn't leave well enough alone. I thought I was never going to see you again, but still I just had to know everything. I tried to tell you I'm a snoop. I tried to warn you.'

Her voice faded as her mind skittered, wondering if she in fact wanted him to hate her for it, or if she wished she could take the words back. Had she known from the second they had met that it would come to this? Had she thought so little of herself that she'd read his blog in an effort to sabotage the relationship from the outset?

His throat worked as the news went down. A million thoughts flickered across his eyes as he obviously thought through the pain, the private moments, the intimate details he had revealed to his computer diary. She stared into his eyes, trying to figure him out, but his thoughts passed too quickly for her to catch.

A storm was gathering and it blew hot tropical air in its wake, rustling at the willow branches above them. The breeze may as well have been Arctic for what it was doing to Siena. With each passing second, Siena's skin grew cold and nothing could prevent the chill enveloping her. She trembled, her chest ached, and the hairs on the backs of her arms stood to attention.

'You read my blog,' he finally said.

'All of it.' There was no point in lying to him any more. He could hardly think worse of her.

'That first night?'

'And since.'

He went pink. 'My fault for leaving the damn thing open. Kane could have seen it.'

The moonlight had disappeared behind a bank of dark grey storm clouds and James's eyes were too dark and hooded for her to have a clue how far back from her he had pulled emotionally.

But then the edge of his eye twitched and for a brief second she thought he might actually have been smiling! But how could he? Oughtn't he to be mortified, angry, ready to tell her exactly what sort of terrible person she was?

But no. That was Rick. The Rick of old. And he'd only been that way out of circumstance and frustration and youth and mixed-up love.

There it was again! The crease in his cheek

had joined the eye twitch. He *was* smiling. James was actually smiling to hear that she had gone behind his back and read his personal diary. How could he possibly be happy that she had done this?

But then she ought to have known that James would be different. Because James *was* different. Different enough from every man she had ever known that he made her feel more, and want more, and desire more from her life than she ever had before.

She suddenly wanted to throw herself into his arms and not let go. But she couldn't. Not yet. No matter how far her hopes and desires had taken her over in these last few days, her conditioning was still fighting against them.

'Since we are confessing tonight,' he said, and Siena had the feeling he had moved even closer to her than he had been earlier.

She moved ever so slightly backward and her back bumped against the solid willow trunk.

'Now is probably the time to let you know that I listened in at the door when you were talking to Kane about your mum.'

Before she could stop herself she let forth a great bellowing, self-aggrandising, 'You *what*?'

She bit her lip, waiting for the noise to stop echoing in the suburban cul-de-sac.

He laughed so hard he had to lean his hand beside her head on the tree trunk. It was a great rolling uproarious laugh that she felt rumbling through her.

Siena thought back on all the things she had said to Kane, about her own private hopes and fears and self-doubt, and how much she had revealed about her elevated feelings for James.

No wonder he had come with flowers!

'You were eavesdropping?' she asked, her indignation obvious. 'And remember you snooped through my PDA that first day too! I should have seen this coming.'

But James only laughed again. 'You think you have any right to complain? You read my private blog. That's way worse than eaves-dropping. Fifty, sixty per cent worse, at least.'

He was right. They were just as bad as each other. Made for each other…

She shook her head and realised his hand

was still resting beside her head. If she tipped her face sideways she would be able to snuggle into his strong wrist.

'My reasons were altruistic,' she said, her stubbornness fading as she felt the chill seep from her bones as his natural warmth enveloped her.

'Mine weren't,' he said, his eyes now filled with a fire she had never seen there before.

And, pretty certain that she wasn't in her right mind any more, she dropped the hand holding the bouquet to her side, reached up with her spare hand, grabbed a handful of his blue sweater and pulled him hard towards her.

It felt as though James had been waiting his whole life for this moment—the moment this woman was able to get past her stubbornness to make the first move.

He leaned in without resistance, his lips crushing against hers, hot, insistent, dissolving him from the inside out. Her skin was so soft and creamy, she tasted of toothpaste and heat.

Her other hand crept around his neck, dangling his now squished roses down his back as she pulled him closer and closer still, pressing her body against his. He pressed back and felt her breasts crushed against his chest.

Oh, Lord. She had nothing on beneath that soft top of hers. He took her around the waist, so thin, his hand burning against the hot skin of her lower back, his little finger diving beneath the elastic of those hot red pyjama bottoms.

She reached higher on tiptoe. Without those insane red high heels of hers she was so small. So delicate. So fine…

His whole body thrummed with excitement that they were actually together, and not just together, but kissing like he hadn't since he was an oversexed teenager.

He stole a hand behind her head, diving into those tempting curls as he had wanted to since that first afternoon. He held her, gentle yet uncompromising. She was exactly where he wanted her, and he was sure that she couldn't have pulled away from his loose grip for all the world.

He buzzed—until he realised that so did his pocket.

'Your phone…' Siena murmured against his lips.

'Ignore it.' He trailed kisses along the edge of her mouth, but he knew she was already pulling back.

'James…' she said, the word torn from her as she did what he couldn't and pushed a hand against his chest, breaking the last tenuous strands of their luxurious embrace.

He stepped back, took a deep breath, rubbed a frustrated hand over his hair, then dived into his pocket for his phone.

'It's home,' he said, his face contorting into a tight frown. What was Kane up to now?

But it was a message from Matt asking him to bring home milk.

He grinned. Matt had joked he would send a message in case James needed an out if it all went horribly wrong. Who knew that the message would come just as it had all been going so very right?

'You should go,' Siena said, her voice ghostly soft.

And James's grin faded. It took some effort

to look into her eyes as, for some reason, for the briefest of seconds, he thought she meant for ever.

'Go?' he repeated.

She nodded, her eyes wide and skittish.

He bit back a growl of frustration. He'd thought that they were finally on the same page, but she was looking at him not like he was the answer to all her dreams but more like the big brick wall in their way.

He took in a deep breath, centred himself, then took her spare hand in his. It was limp and unusually cool. He could feel she was shivering. He wanted nothing more than to drag her into his arms and not let go, but somehow he didn't think that would help.

He had to be honest. To stop playing word games and tell her outright why he had come to her.

'Siena, I have come here tonight to ask you to tell Max you can't go to Rome. I would like you to stay.' *Here goes…* 'Stay for me. Let's see how this thing between us could develop with some real time invested in it.'

Her eyes blinked up at him, moist and wide.

She swallowed, her thin throat obviously working hard.

'That's it?' she finally asked.

Well, now, that wasn't quite the reaction he'd been expecting. He'd thought himself indescribably brave in laying himself on the line like that.

But if she wanted more from him he wasn't quite sure he had more to give, because even though Matt had told him to think about himself for once, he feared it would never be just about him.

What if she stayed and this thing between them never got off the ground? It would be his fault that she'd given up her dream job.

What if she stayed but was not looking for anything more than a fling and Kane became even more attached to her before she figured that out?

What if he thought he was ready for her, and found down the track that he wasn't as strong as he thought he was? What if his feelings for her weren't enough?

Or, just the opposite, what if they stayed together but his need for her always outweighed her need for him. Could he live like that? He knew that Dinah had always felt that way, but she had Kane to think about. But, now he was in the same shoes, could he?

'That's it,' he said, his spine stiffening. 'It's the best I can offer you right now.'

Oh, God. He was trying.

Siena could see that. He was making her the best offer he could. It was a really sensible offer. For any regular girl, any together girl, it was a lovely offer.

But for this girl it wasn't enough.

She loved James. She had fallen hard for his gentleness, his tenderness and his kindness and his wish to see the best in a bad situation.

But the problem was, he was the one who had started her thinking that she deserved more in the first place.

'You asked if I was a huffer as a kid,' she said, biting her lip so as to stop the completely irrational feeling that she was about to cry. 'I *still* am a huffer, James. I've lived my own life for so long I am set in my ways. I'm stubborn. I'm a pain in the butt. And, just like Rick has said, I'm a born nomad. So thank you for your really sweet offer. But I'm afraid that it's only the second best offer I've had this weekend.'

She was lying through her teeth. She knew it the minute the words left her mouth. His offer was so tempting it terrified her. She was so interested she could feel a definite wobble beginning in the region of her lower lip, especially when faced with the expression on James's face. With every word she said his face closed down, all semblance of the smile evaporating until she wondered if she had only ever imagined it.

James was ready to call her bluff, to blurt out that he didn't believe a word she was saying. The tears brimming in her eyes, the passion with which she had kissed him, even his own heart told him she was lying.

But there was no single logical reason he could think of why she would.

'Right,' he said, backing away. He glanced at his watch, not even seeing the face. 'It's late, so I should head back.'

He'd said what he'd come to say. He had bared his feelings for her as much as a simple cabinet maker without all that much experience in these matters could.

He'd brought her flowers, he'd thrown stones against her window, he'd told her that he'd thought of little but her since they'd met, he'd even felt himself lose a little bit of his soul to her when they had kissed.

But she didn't want him.

A set of car lights hit them both, bathing Siena in a beam of light that showed her breathing was heavy, she clutched his roses to her chest so tightly her knuckles had gone white, her hair was a mass of curls and her lips were swollen from his kiss.

For a brief second his instincts told him that she loved him right back, but for some crazy reason was sending him away anyway. It took all of James's strength not to haul her over his shoulder and drag her back to his place so he could spend the night showing her why she was wrong and he was right.

But then a fat drop of rain landed on the back

of his neck. Followed by another and another. The storm had arrived and he had about twenty seconds to get back to the car before he would be drenched.

He took another step away and it felt as if he'd walked a mile. 'Goodnight, Siena.'

He waited for her to give him something, to tell him why she had told Kane he was the greatest man she had known, to reciprocate his feelings, to grab him by the shirt-front with as much passion as she had only moments before…

But her lips did not move, even to tell him goodbye.

And, with that, he turned and walked away, his eyes blurred by more than the sudden driving rain.

Siena's throat was clogged with fear and love and confusion and self-recrimination as she watched James run through the belting rain, get into his car and drive away.

She'd let him go. She'd actually been strong enough to let him go.

Well, she wasn't going to get a minute of

sleep that night so at least she had hours ahead of her to beat herself up about it.

The sudden tropical shower died enough for her to make a quick dash for the house. She kept running, up the stairs and into her room, where she threw herself on to her lumpy bed.

Her poor flowers looked even worse for wear than when he had given them to her. More had lost their petals and some had lost their heads completely. She didn't blame them. She felt as though she'd lost hers days ago.

As she twirled them about she noticed there was a card attached. Curiosity got the better of her, as always, and she opened it to find a copy of the photo that had been taken of them on the Skyrail when they had smiled at the frog. He must have bought it on the sly when she'd been browsing in the gift shop for a present for the twins.

As she stared into the photo, in its silly rainforest-inspired cardboard frame, two single tears spilled from her misty eyes and down her hot cheeks.

In the photo she was leaning into James,

smiling wider than she had ever known herself to smile.

And James only had eyes for her.

CHAPTER TEN

ONE o'clock Saturday afternoon, Siena sat by Max's pool in the same seat in which she had sat merely twenty-four hours before.

After sleeping not a wink the night before as she had stayed up finding a way through the fog to see what she really wanted her future to entail, the only thing keeping her awake was nervous tension.

'So?' Max said, watching her over the top of a Martini. 'What will it be, Siena? Do you plan to continue rising to the top in taking the Rome position or are you going to be like the majority of my girls and let real life get in the way of a good thing?'

'Neither, Max,' Siena said, her voice sounding a heck of a lot stronger than she felt. She was about to take the biggest gamble of her life and she had no idea if she could pull it off.

But all the sacrifices she had ever made of her time, and her loyalty to the company, and most importantly the reward at the end, would make taking the biggest chance of her life worth it.

'Max, I have an offer to make you I think you can't refuse.'

His eyes narrowed. 'I thought my remuneration package for the Rome gig was fairly unbeatable.'

'And it was. But it's not the package that concerns me. I want…I need to be here. Not Rome. I need to stay in Cairns.'

Max watched her over the rim of his glass before he sighed and ran a ringed hand across his temple. 'Oh, Lord, if you tell me you've met a boy I'll drown myself in my Martini right now.'

'I wouldn't want you to do that, Max. But I'm afraid I have met a boy.'

Max rolled his eyes. 'If only one could hire eunuchs with the talent you girls have. But alas. It seems that, having a mostly female workforce, I will continue to lose my favourite girls to family.'

'But that's just my point. You don't have to lose me, Max. I just think you could use me in a way that suits both of us.' She pulled a piece of paper out of her handbag with a shaking hand. 'May I?'

He waved a flamboyant hand her way, allowing her to continue.

It would mean less pay, it would mean more hours, and it would mean that never again would she have to push a ridiculously heavy drinks trolley down an aeroplane aisle while wearing heels at thirty thousand feet.

It meant that she would have to find herself a permanent base in Cairns instead of a tiny serviced apartment in Melbourne that merely served as somewhere to store the hoards of clothes she was partial to collecting on her European stopovers.

But that was fine with her. Because it meant that she could also make James a counter offer to the one he had made the night before, which she hoped would be too good for him to refuse as well.

It was time to stop running. And, as she had sat watching the sun rise from Rick's back porch that morning, she realised that she already had.

She set out to tell Max what her new job would entail, with all the confidence in the world that he would then blithely fire her on the spot for daring to presume that she knew more about his business than he did.

James sat in his studio, looking out over the large square garden of his suburban home.

It felt too quiet. It was Saturday yet Kane wasn't home to help him out in his workshop as he usually did. Cate and Dave had called that morning to ask if Kane wanted to come with them and their kids to the Cairns lagoon for the day. And without hesitation his shy, quiet son had actually smiled and said, 'Can I?'

He stared at his mobile phone, which sat silent and still on his workbench.

Dust fluttered slowly through a ray of sunlight. Siena ought to have finished with Max ages ago. In the last hour he had see-sawed through moments in which, despite her insistence that she didn't want to stay for him, he was hopeful she had told her boss to shove the Rome job, and others where he was just as sure she had done as she had always intended and taken the job and run.

Either way, after she had let him leave without saying a word the night before, he was all but certain he was not on the list of those she would be calling with the news.

But, even after the way they had left things, he *needed* to know.

He loved her. Having lived a night with the thought that he might never see her again, he knew that he loved her more now than ever. His love for her filled him up, brought him pleasure and pain, and he wouldn't have traded either for the world. And because he loved her he wanted her to be happy. Sure, he would prefer her to be happy with him, but if she had to leave…

He slammed a fist against his workbench. Damn it! If only he'd said things differently the night before. Told her more of his feelings. Kissed her longer. Refused to let her go.

Never before had he felt that something so important was so far out of his control. His whole life had been about control—controlling his feelings, his actions, his wife, his son's temperament. But this, the most important moment in his life to date, was not his to decide.

Feeling uninspired to work, as if his heavy limbs couldn't be trusted to construct even the most basic design, he instead opened his blog.

To say goodbye? To post a final entry? It felt like the right time to say enough was enough.

Even though he had learnt a hell of a lot more than he bargained for in taking on Siena Capuletti and her roller coaster ride of a change of scene, he had to be thankful that she had helped him complete that important stage of his life.

From now on he knew he had friends who would happily talk through his concerns. Matt. Mandy. Dave and Cate. His blog had served its purpose but it no longer had a place in his life.

His fingers paused over the keyboard as he

searched for a way to say goodbye. But, before he typed a word, he noticed that some time that morning someone had left a comment against his most recent post.

He'd never had a comment before. That was probably one of the main reasons why he had continued with it for so long, because he'd thought nobody had been paying it any attention.

His hand hovered over the mouse, but curiosity won in the end and he clicked on the comment box. And then his throat closed over completely as he read the words on the page.

Saturday, 8:12am
Two days ago I met a boy.

I hadn't been actively looking to meet one, which is usually when these things happen—in the moment when you are least prepared for them.

For unprepared for him I was.

Until I met this boy I thought I was living the high life. I've visited the Eiffel Tower fifty times. Fifty! I've taken classes to learn how to weld, how to dropkick a guy twice my size and how to trim a bon-sai tree. Why? Because I was independent, self-sufficient and stubbornly determined to remain that way. I could take care of my-self. I needed nobody.

But this boy showed me that my indepen-dence had come at a price. Independence meant isolation. Isolation had turned to loneliness. And he made me ask myself if I was really happy to drift about the ocean of life alone forever more.

And the answer?

No. I'm not. Because, since I have known this boy, I have discovered that I was never an island. I was merely a lonely soul adrift but now I have found where my home really is.

I only hope that I have not left it too late to tell him how much this has meant to me.

I understand why he might see me as too much hard work, because believe it, I am, and I understand that after last night he might not believe that I was only trying to do what was best for him, and for the son he loves so much, but I'm telling him how I feel all the same.

If he can ever forgive me for being slow on the uptake, if he is willing to take my scratched and dented heart, if he is able to see his way past my stubbornness, then he, this boy, this man, this man that I love more than anything in the world, more than my independence, more even than Rome and all it represents, he can have me.

Because, now that I know that I want to come home, I realise too that it would never be home unless he was there with me.

S

James let loose a nice loud helpful swear word.

Clinging to the mouse for dear life, he took a deep breath and read the whole message again, just to make sure he wasn't dreaming.

When he finally believed every word to be true, he swore even louder and grabbed for the phone, his hands shaking as directory enquiries put him through to Rick's Body Shop.

'Rick speaking.'

'Rick, it's James Dillon. Is Siena there?'

'No, mate. That crazy-looking driver of hers picked her up to take her to the airport about half an hour ago. She still has to work that flight back to Melbourne. But I thought you—'

James hung up and was out of his chair, into the kitchen, grabbing his car keys and pulling a T-shirt over his bare chest and running down the front path faster than he had ever run before.

Slow Saturday drivers threatened to block his every turn, but somehow gaps in the traffic opened up before him every time he needed them to. Lights turned green upon his insistence. The fates were giving him one last chance to get this right.

As he neared the airport a big baby-blue poster advertising MaxAir caught his attention. And he almost crashed the car as Siena's beautiful smiling face looked back at him.

He slowed, rubbed his eyes, saw that it was really her. She was dressed as a flight attendant in one of those blue suits and matching Jackie O hats, her glorious curls pulled back off her face into a severe bun, a wide smile on her lovely face, her eyes sparkling for all the world to see. Her stunning ocean-green eyes, her fine cheekbones, her heart-shaped face, her—

The car behind him beeped its horn and he pulled away. The poster could wait. If the fates continued to conspire in his favour the real thing could be at the end of the line.

The real thing…

God, he had so much to tell her and this time he was going to tell her right.

He'd left the night before thinking he'd said all he had gone to her to say. But after reading her love letter to him, for that was what it had been, he knew that he'd been holding back.

Damn it! He could have blown it all.

If she hadn't have been brave enough, and sensitive enough, to see through the superficial things like roses and throwing pebbles against her window, and tenuous offers to *give it a go and see what happened* he could have lost her.

He sailed over a speed hump as he drove into the short-term car park, found a spot and landed on the pavement running, thankful that he had remote central locking or he would have left the damn car to its own devices.

Pushing past tourists with baggage trolleys and families slowly wandering into the terminal to pick up loved ones, he rushed along the length of the outdoor car park.

He wanted to be with this woman for the rest of his life. He loved her stubbornness and the fact that she was hard work and that she made Kane laugh and made him smile. He loved the fact that she was sure, and that their courtship had weathered storms a-plenty and come out the other side stronger. And he loved the fact that she loved him right on back. That part he loved most of all.

But he hadn't told her any of that.

Instead he'd dangled a carrot and hoped for the best. And now, hours after she had written that note, she could have given up on him and taken the Rome gig and left…

Unable to wait for the electronic doors to slide slowly open, he pushed through a side door of the departure gates. Running backwards, he eyed the monitor showcasing all departing flights until he found the MaxAir flight to Melbourne.

And then he was off, ignoring the packed escalator, taking the steps two at a time and travelling down the long hallway as fast as he could without arousing the attention of airport security.

As he closed in on the departure lounge, he took in the scene around him, willing his senses to slice through the hundreds of travellers to pick up only on her familiar dark curls, the classy scent of her perfume, her soft skin and those winning wilful eyes.

Where else did he find her but sitting in a café, a half-drunk cappuccino sitting congealing at her side, as she concentrated wholeheartedly on the dozen salt packets balanced in a precarious pile before her?

He slowed to a walk, taking advantage of a few moments to watch her, just watch her being her.

Her head was cocked to one side, her dark curls tamed into a slick wavy hairdo reminiscent of a forties movie star, sexy as hell in her baby-blue MaxAir uniform, looking nothing like the robot he had accused her of being all those millennia ago, but very beautiful, and very soft, and very real.

Marring the vision of true incandescence, her stormy green eyes seemed heartbreakingly sad and he guessed that lashings of eyeliner had been used to cover up evidence of tears. Tears he had caused? Tears that made his chest feel tight with regret. Tears he hoped to never let happen again.

Siena. The woman he loved. How had it ever come to this? How he had been lucky enough to find love twice in a lifetime, he had no idea. He'd done something right by somebody to deserve such a blessing. Especially because he knew in his heart that this time it would last a lifetime.

'Siena,' he said, his voice thick with emotion, no longer able to hold back from going to her.

Siena looked up. And she couldn't believe her bloodshot eyes.

'James?'

She'd been sitting there, thinking of nothing but him, wondering if he might find her letter one day, if he ever braved his blog again after her confession that she had read it all, and then there he was. Real. There. Hers.

She rose from her seat, staring into his face—his breathing was ragged, his clothes askew, his eyes bright and vivid and warm and willing.

He stood before her dressed almost the same as he had been that first day, in an old T-shirt, soft jeans clinging to lean hips, heavy scuffed work boots, short ash-brown hair just a little ragged from running his hands across it as he always seemed to do when she was acting a little nuts, which was often enough.

He was absolutely the sexiest, sweetest, most gorgeous man she had ever known. Sexier even than Action James of the photos on top of the piano. She didn't know that man. But this man she knew. *This* man she loved.

Without another word, she rushed to him, wrapping her arms about his neck as he enveloped her completely in his inviolable embrace. Her whole body shook as she let go, let go of all her hurt and pain and happiness and love in one great gushing stream of tears.

Only once her racking sobs had subsided did James pull slowly away, sliding his arms from around her so he could run soft fingers down her damp cheeks.

'What's with all the tears?' he asked, a true smile lighting his beautiful eyes.

Siena sniffed and did her best to take a proper breath. But she couldn't. His very presence had stolen her breath fair away. 'I can't…I can't believe you're really here.'

'Ye of little faith,' he chastised.

'I hoped. I wished. I sent out as many happy thoughts as I could. But I never really thought it would happen.'

'Tell me about it,' he said, now running his hands lovingly over her hair. 'I've spent months thinking those very same thoughts, all but convincing myself I could never possibly hope to feel this way about someone. Now it just pains me to think that if I hadn't got here in time…'

Siena could feel the pain in his voice as he contemplated her leaving and not coming back.

'What?' she said. 'Are you some sort of quitter?'

He raised an eloquent eyebrow, a hint of a sparkle in his eyes.

'Would you not have chased me all the way to Melbourne?' she asked.

He thought about it and then smiled. 'Actually, I would.'

'Well, it's your lucky day. It wouldn't have come to that. I've booked myself on a flight back here tomorrow afternoon as it is.'

'A working flight?' he asked, and she knew he still hadn't realised that she had really gone ahead and chosen him over Rome.

'As a passenger, of course! Because, now that I will be working here, I was thinking I might try to find myself a cute little apartment somewhere up this way. Something with air-conditioning, for sure.'

'Don't tell me you quit,' he said and the sparkle had turned into the beginnings of a smile and Siena knew she was home.

She saw the wheels and cogs turn in his head as he computed what she was telling him.

'Nah,' she said. 'I made Max an offer he couldn't refuse. I was going to tell all when I turned up at your place as a surprise tomorrow night but now you've saved me the trip… I suggested that if he thinks I'm that fabulous at my job that I should stay here training all his new recruits to be just like me, making sure they know what MaxAir service is all about if they want to fly the grand overseas routes. Telling them the truth of it, preparing them for the joy and the sacrifices both. And he thought it a great idea!'

'Of course I believe it. He would have been stupid not to think so. Though they couldn't be just like you if they tried. Not one of them. Unless of course you did build an army of Siena-shaped robots to do the job—'

She glared at him and slapped him on the back. Then, before she knew what he was about to do, he grabbed her tight and twirled her in his arms.

Siena laughed out loud. She felt giddy, loved and wondrous, like someone in one of those romantic ads for telephone companies that made every girl on the planet cry.

He brought her back to the ground, hugging her tight, whispering against her ear. 'Don't get an apartment,' he said, his voice insistent, strong and determined.

'Don't?'

'I meant it when I told you that you should stay. I was just too struck dumb by the image of you in those sexy-as-hell pyjamas to be able to find the words to tell you properly. But since this get-up does nothing at all for me…'

He paused, running his hands over her shoulders and down her back until they were tucked beneath the cropped jacket at her waist, thus utterly negating the words he had just said.

'Siena,' he murmured, loud enough for her ears only, 'sweetheart, stay with me. Live with me. Be with me. Marry me.'

Marry me. Had he really said marry me?

'Did you really say…?'

He slowly brought a hand to either side of her face, making sure she was looking at him, into those deep grey eyes of his. 'Siena, you must know how much I love you.'

I do now, she thought, her mind and heart and soul reeling and tripping and giddy. But instead she said, 'I love you too.'

Then, in one fluid movement, they moved to kiss one another.

And Siena knew that, after all her years of flying the world, she had finally come home.

MILLS & BOON® PUBLISH EIGHT LARGE PRINT TITLES A MONTH. THESE ARE THE EIGHT TITLES FOR MAY 2007

THE ITALIAN'S FUTURE BRIDE
Michelle Reid

PLEASURED IN THE BILLIONAIRE'S BED
Miranda Lee

BLACKMAILED BY DIAMONDS,
BOUND BY MARRIAGE
Sarah Morgan

THE GREEK BOSS'S BRIDE
Chantelle Shaw

OUTBACK MAN SEEKS WIFE
Margaret Way

THE NANNY AND THE SHEIKH
Barbara McMahon

THE BUSINESSMAN'S BRIDE
Jackie Braun

MEANT-TO-BE MOTHER
Ally Blake

V

Detailed info for
teachers on fairy tales
- The revisionist tale
- The Traditionalist tale